DEAD IN PLAIN SIGHT

DEAD IN PLAIN SIGHT

I FEAR NO EVIL™ BOOK FOUR

MARTHA CARR
MICHAEL ANDERLE

DISRUPTIVE IMAGINATION

LMBPN Publishing
PMB 196, 2540 South Maryland Pkwy
Las Vegas, NV 89109

First US edition, July 2018
Version 1.02, September 2018

DEAD IN PLAIN SIGHT TEAM

Thanks to the JIT Readers

John Ashmore
James Caplan
Mary Morris
Daniel Weigert
Peter Manis
Larry Omans
Paul Westman
Micky Cocker

If we've missed anyone, please let us know!

DEDICATIONS

From Martha

To everyone who still believes in magic
and all the possibilities that holds.
To all the readers who make this
entire ride so much fun.
And to my son, Louie and so many wonderful friends who
remind me all the time of what
really matters and how wonderful
life can be in any given moment.

From Michael

To Family, Friends and
Those Who Love
To Read.
May We All Enjoy Grace
To Live The Life We Are
Called.

Shay parked the van on a darkened street a couple of blocks away from the massive wrought-iron fence surrounding their target, an elegant old Victorian mansion.

She sighed and shook her head as she looked over at the young gray elf. It was a hard sell, but Shay eventually relented and let her come on the mission. Somehow Lily had talked Peyton into pitching the idea to Shay, too.

Besides, Shay knew this one was going to be tricky. An extra body along who had some magical abilities could tip the scale.

"Not as cool as your Fiat," said Lily. Lily slipped out of the car, pulling on the slim backpack that had been resting at her feet.

"Stands out far less, especially at night," said Shay.

Shay grabbed a pair of binoculars from behind the front seat. Getting spotted wearing AR goggles would be hard to explain.

She snickered. "I'll just tell everyone we're practicing for a movie role. Spies who bird watch. At night."

"This is L.A. They'd not only believe you, they'd want to steal the idea."

"And ask for a part." Shay smiled, surprising herself. Missions of any kind required focus, not that Shay wasn't aware of every nearby movement. But she was actually having *fun*... Fun without shooting someone. That was new.

She still wondered if her big experiment with having a life could end up being great short term and hazardous for her longevity.

"You remember your part?" Shay crouched down as they got closer to the edge of the small estate. Lily took a similar stance not too far from her.

"Keep an eye on the perimeter."

"And?"

"Don't get killed, I remember. That one's kind of a given."

"And yet, Peyton forgets it all the time."

"I heard that." His voice inside Shay's head came to life.

Lily let out a snicker as she moved forward, taking her position a few yards ahead near the tall iron fence. The gray elf's twitch reflexes were going to come in handy on this mission. Her speed at learning small weaponry had been impressive.

"I made it clear. Audio blackout during this op," whispered Shay.

"Quit baiting me, then." The sound of a cat yowling and something falling and hitting the floor could be heard through the earpiece. "Oh shit."

Shay took out the earpiece and slipped it into a small pocket on her jacket. That was too much of a distraction. She could find out later what broke and take it out of Peyton's share.

Shadows shifted in the sky above the mansion, accompanied by a distant buzz, proof of at least one security drone. A couple of suited men wandered the perimeter. Shay couldn't be sure how many more might be inside, but the drone's thermal scans thirty minutes prior suggested at least two interior guards.

"Pretty arrogant, Colonel Grayson," Shay muttered. "Your cockiness is going to cost you tonight."

His company, Grayson PMC Services, might claim they were legitimate military contractors, but they worked more as ruthless mercenaries for criminals. They'd made a lot of enemies. People like Shay.

She lowered her binoculars. Or maybe they hadn't. Maybe the only person they'd ever pissed off enough to go after them was her.

But that was more than enough.

The tomb raider retrieved a small azure crystal orb out of her pocket. Dark bands swirled slowly on the surface. Using her other hand, she pulled a note out of her pocket and snorted at the awful handwriting. The gnome's scrawl looked like it had been written by a panicked chicken.

"Come on, Tubal-Cain. Can't you use some magic to improve your handwriting?"

"Let's do this," said Lily, anxious to erase the last mission and the Ice Witch from her memory.

The instructions from the gnome reinforced that the artifact should be simple enough to use. She only needed to wrap her hand around the orb, say the control phrase, and hold it tightly. Once she let go, it'd automatically deactivate.

The gnome had made her practice pronouncing the short phrase for fifteen minutes in his shop. Shay didn't recognize the language—not that she was an expert on spoken Oriceran languages. The fact that the gnome had refused to clarify what it meant didn't help.

Probably calling to some dark and ancient Oriceran god for help.

One last comment in the instructions caught her eye.

Magic is alive, unlike human technology. Be careful about misusing the artifact. Everything has consequences.

"Consequences, huh?" Shay whispered. She shook her head and slipped on a ski mask and gloves as Lily did the same, hiding her long gray hair. It was time to execute the plan.

Shay pocketed the artifact and kept moving slowly forward. "Misuse" was a nebulous concept, but the night's mission wasn't about theft or murder—or at least that wasn't the plan.

I'm trying to stop more people from dying. That's not misuse. Sure, I'm the one who'd be killing them, but I'm going out of my way to try to prevent that. In a sense, I'm saving their lives.

Shay smirked at the thought, but her mirth vanished when she remembered why she was there.

Grayson was sniffing too close to Alison for Shay's comfort. She might have scared them off for a while by killing their men in Virginia, but a direct message to their leader would ensure the girl would be safe.

The tomb raider clung to the shadows between the

sparse street lights. The advantage of her target living on a ritzy street was that the local homeowners valued aesthetics more than brightly-lit streets at night.

"For a mercenary, this guy's kind of a dumbass about security," whispered Lily.

"It's always the low-tech that saves people in the end. Remember that."

Shay brought up an app on her phone, her finger hovering over a button marked 'Engage' as she closed on the fence.

Need to time this just right.

She pressed the button and pocketed her phone...and no dramatic shouts followed. The drones didn't crash. It had gone just as she'd planned.

Lily gave her a thumbs up and Shay watched as Lily easily clambered over the fence in two moves and onto the other side, barely touching the fence.

Shay was going to need a more conventional method that still got the job done.

Shay charged a corner of the fence under the deep shadows of a tall willow tree, her heart rate kicking up. The next few seconds would determine if she could get inside without having to shoot people. The guards were on the opposite side of the house, giving her a few minutes' window to gain entry without having to use the artifact.

The tomb raider leapt for the fence, vaulting over and landing with a grin. Four moves, not bad. Even better, no alarms.

Peyton's security program was working perfectly. He'd gotten the idea from Shay after she'd revealed the Warehouse Three Annex and told him how she'd fooled him by showing him false footage. He'd started working on a program to dynamically spoof a variety of security feeds.

It wasn't the first time he'd seen or used the technique, but his experience with the Annex had convinced him that the concept was more powerful than he'd believed. The male ego was a powerful motivator.

The program might not be much help in some hidden Templar maze beneath an Aldi supermarket in Munich, but it was more than proving its worth now.

Shay moved away from the gate, as Lily gave the signal that all was clear and Shay gave a return signal. Lily gave a nod and moved to the left under the short canopy of the ornamental trees that bordered the property.

Even though the grounds were dark, like any elf, Lily could see the magical energy that told her someone was magical. Very useful.

Shay darted toward the house, keeping her head down as she made for a side door. The door cracked open, dim light spilling out.

The tomb raider yanked the orb out of her pocket and whispered the activation phrase. The artifact warmed in her hand, becoming uncomfortably hot but not burning her skin. She stopped and held her breath.

A guard emerged from the house with a yawn and looked right at her.

Let's see how good you are, gnome.

The guard didn't react or give any indication he'd seen Shay. He closed the door, tapped a lock code into its keypad, and walked toward the back of the house.

Shay stared at the guard for a few long moments before looking down at her body. Invisibility was easy to understand, but she was neither invisible nor in some strange alternate plane of existence. She was there and visible, but the guard acted like she wasn't.

"People's minds are easy to trick," the gnome had told her. "Give them any excuse to look away, and they will. This artifact gives them that excuse. Metal toys don't have minds to trick, so it does nothing for them. You'll have to take care of that sort of thing yourself."

The tomb raider shook her head and walked to the keypad. She tapped in the code Peyton had hacked the house security system for earlier, and when the door clicked open she hurried inside the darkened home.

Shay kept her grip on the artifact as she sauntered with a grin down the hall and up the stairs. A turn brought her to the master bedroom. The door creaked opened, and she stepped inside and closed it.

The mercenary leader slept peacefully on his back, his weathered face speaking to years of hard living. Shay rolled her eyes at the decades-younger voluptuous blonde who slept next to him.

The tomb raider-turned-home invader slipped the artifact back in her pocket before pulling one of her adamantine knives out its sheath.

Colonel Grayson's eyes snapped open when she touched the blade to his throat.

Shay lifted a finger to her mouth and shushed him. "Quiet."

The man's face tightened in anger and defiance. "I won't beg. If you're going to do it, then do it." He kept his voice low, as if he didn't want to wake his trophy wife before his execution.

Shay wasn't sure if she was impressed or annoyed.

"Nah," she whispered.

He blinked. "Excuse me?"

"If this were about killing you, you'd already be dead, and I wouldn't have bothered with all this bullshit sneaking around. This is about sending a message that will result in less trouble for a young woman."

"Okay, what message? And what girl?" He still sounded too comfortable to suit Shay.

Shay leaned forward and kept the knife at the man's throat. "It's come to my attention that two of your men were poking around in Virginia, looking for a girl. You're gonna stay the fuck away from that girl, as are your men."

"Are you the one who butchered my men?"

She let a chuckle escape. "I'm just a person who has an interest in making sure that girl lives a happy life without mercenaries fucking with her."

The wife stirred in her sleep. If she woke up and started screaming, things might get unpleasant for everyone involved.

Just stay asleep. Your only crime was marrying a dick.

Colonel Grayson's jaw tightened. That's better, thought Shay.

"Who the fuck are you, really?" he asked. "A bodyguard? Part of some sort of protection agency? Who the fuck is that girl that she has that kind of protection?"

"You don't need to know that."

He snorted. "My people looked into that girl. We know she's linked to Brownstone, but we found nothing about any sort of security firm."

Shay shook her head. The asshole was going to keep the strongman front, even though she had a knife to his throat.

"Let's just say I'm a guardian angel in black, Colonel Grayson. One who gained access to your bedroom despite all your security and guards," Shay added as she removed her knife.

The man jerked up, and Shay snapped her arm forward again. He froze in place when the tip of her blade pricked his throat and drew a single drop of blood.

Shay tsked. "You are hopelessly outclassed, asshole. You that eager to die? I'm trying not to kill anyone, but I'm not married to the idea."

Grayson gritted his teeth and didn't respond.

"Shouldn't have done that. Might have woken up wifey-poo over there." Shay glanced over at his wife. "What? You have...twenty years on her? Thirty years? Or did you find a bunch of money for beautification magic?"

Shay heard the sound of guards moving across the lawn outside and knew her time was drawing short. No need to test Lily's skills too much on her first day back in the field.

Shay pressed the tip of the blade. "The only reason I'm not slitting your throat right now is the small, small chance that it'd lead to some unfortunate police investigation or some shit like that. This is your final warning, though. Next time you die." She grinned. "And don't think your big plan to hire a few magical mercs and overpay for some shitty magical artifact is gonna help you. They wouldn't be the first magic users I've killed. Or the second. Or the third."

Shay took a step back, her gaze still locked on the man.

Grayson glared at her. "How do you know about that? Only my top-level men know about that."

"I'll let you stew on that and figure it out yourself."

"Fuck, you're in my personal files."

"Something like that." Shay gave him a little mocking salute. Peyton's ability to break in to any files and Lily's talent at seeing magical trails and following them were proving to be very valuable assets to her operations.

"Have a good evening, Colonel. Sleep well, for now."

She made her way back the same way she came in and found Lily at the rendezvous point, sweaty and smiling from ear to ear.

"Just tell me, did you leave any evidence behind?"

"Not a bit. It was just a few guards and they never saw me coming. They're taking a nap. This was fun."

"Kid, you may have really found your calling."

Shay pushed into the main room of Warehouse Five, the lights above clicking on in succession. She passed through several shelves filled with random knick-knacks, most of which were of no value. Many were holdovers from when she'd first purchased the place, and she'd kept them to act as decoys for anyone who penetrated the warehouse.

A random warehouse invader might, for example, mistake a Franklin Mint Civil War Chess Set for a magical artifact, or commemorative plates from the 2028 election. She passed a stack of bright children's books with stylized images of elves, dwarves, gnomes, and something that looked like a walking giant rat. A Willen, if she remembered correctly. She'd never actually seen one.

Shay checked the title. *Our New Friends from Oriceran: A Kid's Guide to our Magical Neighbors.*

She snickered.

Friends? Even most humans aren't friends of other humans.

Shay continued toward a wall in the back and ignored the other decoy items, including several shelves of translucent crystals and strange weathered brass contraptions she'd purchased from a local artist.

It wasn't paranoia; it was practicality. The contents of Warehouses One through Three would be expensive to replace, but it'd at least be possible. The rare book collection of Warehouse Four and the artifacts stored in Warehouse Five could be lost forever if she weren't careful. She hadn't even told Peyton the locations of Warehouses Four and Five.

Peyton thought he was being clever and had narrowed down the possible locations of the high-value book and artifact warehouses, but the man had no clue where they really were, and as much as the tomb raider had come to trust him, that was how she intended to keep it. He was smart and resourceful, but he'd crack like an egg under torture.

People could say what they wanted, but sometimes security by obscurity was a good strategy.

Lily on the other hand, she was another story. If she wanted to, she could follow the trail a retrieved artifact left and find Warehouse Five. Still, the way she'd kept the hidden part of the Annex to herself and didn't tell Peyton was impressive.

A non-descript wall stopped Shay's movement, and she placed her palm on a hidden pad near the center. She hissed at the burn of the DNA scan, then leaned forward for the retinal one. A keypad popped up and she tapped in her passphrase.

The wall parted with a loud groan, revealing a large hidden chamber with floor-to-ceiling gray metal shelving on one side and dark wooden shelving on the other. One could never know how a magical artifact might react to its environment.

Nothing looked disturbed. If Lily had been there to take a look around, she was careful not to move anything.

A small case filled with the magical artifacts Shay had found at Alison's house when she was helping clean it out sat near the entrance. The girl didn't want them for now, so Shay was content to let them sit and gather dust. They weren't hers to use, and she hadn't even bothered doing much in the way of research on them.

A velvet-and-wood case containing a set of porcelain cups whose cracks had been repaired with gold rested on one of the wooden shelves. They were magical *kintsugi* cups that could filter poison from drinks. Not exactly something that was all that tactically useful, but she didn't feel the need to sell them, either.

Her alien stone from Mexico lay comfortably in a small glass case near the cups.

Past the shelves, a rack for clothes stood next to a weapons rack. Shay lacked any current magical outfits, but a long, curved sword hung from the latter, a Masamune *tachi*. The enchanted blade was powerful enough to get through even Brownstone's amulet-enhanced skin, though not small enough for easy concealment. She'd save it for when she knew she'd be going up against someone powerful and magical.

Someone like Yulia Solokova. Shay still owed the witch for Antarctica and for Lily's father. She ground her teeth at the memory of her icy humiliation.

Whatever. We'll both get our chance eventually.

Shay pulled the gnome's orb from her pocket and laid it on a soft cushion. It'd be safe in her vault until she could return it. The gnome was out of town for a while. She hadn't dared ask him where he might be going.

The artifact had made her entrance and escape from Grayson's mansion easy. Depending on some strange gnome to help her, or even Peyton or Lily, still sat a bit uneasily on her stomach, but the little adventure's success proved why it was a good idea.

I might be good, but I know when to bring in help.

Shay blew out a breath. She'd taken care of one part of her new family in protecting Alison, and soon it'd be time to look into the girl's soon-to-be adoptive father. She still had a lot of questions about Brownstone, including the nature of his amulet.

The tomb raider let out a quiet snicker. Between Brownstone and the weird alien crap, she was surrounded by mysteries that didn't look profitable.

So much for my original life plan.

2

Shay was clicking away on the computer in the Warehouse Two office when Peyton rolled in, right on time. She had already dropped Lily off at Warehouse One for a workout to give her a chance to talk to Peyton, alone.

There were a few things he needed to be aware of, and it was as good a time as any to talk to him about them. She'd hoped Brownstone could stay out of trouble, but just in the days since her little adventure at Grayson's house things had grown more complicated.

All of these distractions were keeping her from her commitments at the college. It had been well over a month since she'd stepped into her role as an adjunct professor and given a lecture.

No time at all to even research any history lessons that were thought to be myth and conveniently turned out to be magic. Her favorite topic.

Still… maybe she could at least squeeze in a stop at

Warehouse Four and find a good book to read. She'd send a quick email while she was thinking of it and at least let them know she was alive. Little did they know that wasn't a given.

"Good morning, Shay," Peyton offered with a bright smile. As usual, his fashion sense remained eclectic at best. Today's outfit included jeans and a T-shirt with a leather vest decorated with a Grateful Dead skull on the back and tall leather military boots laced up the front.

Shay stepped out of the office and leaned against the wall, her arms crossed. "I see you're figuring out how to get to work on time and still make sure no one is following you. I don't know if it's your crazy random street algorithm, but whatever works."

Peyton grinned. "Glad you approve."

She gestured toward his clothes. "And…this is an interesting new look. I always pegged you more for an upscale hipster, rather than… Well, whatever the hell this is."

Peyton scoffed. "You can't put my style in a box or reduce it to mere labels. I'm a chameleon, and I can blend in anywhere if I want." A thoughtful look passed over his face. "Maybe that should be my new alias."

"Chameleon?"

"Yeah."

Shay rolled her eyes. "Why don't you focus on getting me a new job instead of worrying about nicknames and aliases?"

"Okay, *Aletheia*."

"That's not the same thing. I use the alias for safety, not to make some sort of statement about my fashion preferences."

Peyton shrugged. "Just sayin'. You've got a cool alias based on the Greek Goddess of Truth, so a new name for me wouldn't hurt."

"Call yourself what you want. Doesn't mean *I'm* gonna call you that."

"Fair enough. You didn't buy that Lily told us her real name, did you? That girl's way too street smart to offer up a nugget of truth like that. Lily is her alias."

"I take it you've been trying to find a trail online."

"And there's nothing. No school records, no social media. She's a gray ghost. Oooh, that would be a good handle."

"Let it go. She'll tell us more when she's ready. And about the gig…"

Peyton gave her a thumb's up. "The Chameleon always does a thorough job."

Shay groaned. "Whatever." She rubbed the back of her neck and frowned. "There's some shit you should know about. It doesn't directly affect you, but it's gonna affect me."

"There's a lot of shit I should know about. Is this about a job?"

The tomb raider shook her head. "Nope, it's about Brownstone."

"What about him?"

"I was poking around on some of the old dark web killer forums, that kind of thing."

Peyton frowned. "Why?"

"To keep an eye out for people who might be trying to kill us."

He waved a hand. "I've got all that stuff automated."

Shay shook her head. "Algorithms can never replace people."

Peyton's eyes widened. "Wait. Are you saying someone's coming for you? Shit. Or *me?*"

"Nope, not yet."

"Then what?"

"They are coming for Brownstone."

Peyton let out a sigh of relief. "Oh. That's no big deal."

"*No big deal?*"

"Come on, Shay. That guy is like a black hole for trouble. I wouldn't be surprised if some country ends up declaring war on him at the rate he's going, and he conquers it and renames it 'Brownstoneland.'"

Shay barked a laugh. "Shit. You're right, and, yeah, more trouble. The Harriken didn't get the message from his last slaughter-fest. They're bringing in help."

"But they already did with that bounty."

"Nope, this time they're putting out enough money to get platinum-grade killers, not random assholes off the street. That means major trouble is probably coming his way."

Peyton looked her up and down with a curious glint in his eye. "And you're going to help him?"

"Yeah, probably." She shrugged. "No big deal. He's pretty convenient to have around."

"I don't get why you don't want to admit you're into the guy. If I batted for the other team, *I'd* be into the guy. He's a total badass. He's the emperor of all badasses."

Peyton withered under Shay's glare.

"The point is, keep an eye out. I'm guessing this is going to end with me killing a bunch of people."

"You? Not Brownstone?"

"That too, but he's a bounty hunter, not a former killer. I think like a hitman, and that's not all."

Peyton shook his head and stepped into the office to sit at the desk, tossing one of Lily's new t-shirts toward a pile of her clothes. "Is there some other international criminal gang sending guys after him?"

"Not yet, but that's not the thing I'm worried about."

"What then?"

Shay hesitated, caught in a rare moment of self-doubt about whether she should be discussing Brownstone's background with Peyton.

"I had a chat with James," she continued after a moment. "Look, the thing is, the guy's too badass not to be magical, and he's got some sort of artifact that makes him even more badass."

"So? That's not a big deal. You've got artifacts too." Peyton rolled his eyes. "Even though you hide them all from me in Warehouse Five."

Shay smirked. "We all have our secrets. Except for you, of course."

"Even from the guy who regularly helps save your life? I would if I could figure out how to keep them."

"*Especially* from the guy who helps save my life." She uncrossed her arms. "And it's not just about artifacts. He's kind of strange looking, and he doesn't even remember where he's from. He just remembers being in the jungle somewhere else and then suddenly in Los Angeles."

Peyton's brow furrowed. "What do you mean?"

"It sounds to me like he gated from some jungle on Oriceran to Earth when he was a little kid."

"Brownstone's Oriceran? But he would have been over here before all that came out."

Shay shrugged. "So? Oricerans were over here before we knew about them. Lily's ancestors, for one. All over the place doing all sorts of shit—mowing their lawns, bowling, working at Wendy's. Whatever."

"Bowling?" Peyton gave her a skeptical look. "Working at Wendy's?"

"They're just examples. The point is, they've always been here, so they've always been able to send people here —like probably Brownstone."

Peyton shook his head. "He might just be a guy whose parents were on a local wizard's good side."

"Maybe. Anyway, I'm going to research his amulet and see what it turns up. At this point, verifying he's from Oriceran would be less weird than finding out that I grabbed a weird alien stone from some possessed elf."

"You want me to look into Brownstone?"

Shay shook her head. "You stick to the alien shit, I'll handle the Oriceran stuff. There's too much weirdness on either side for one person. And Peyton…"

"Don't tell Lily. Not hard to figure out. You normally keep a pretty good eye on that teenager and you left her alone in a warehouse. By now, if you had any secrets in that one, she's found them."

"This whistling while you work isn't so bad," Peyton mumbled to himself after finishing a whistled ditty.

Working for Shay had started out as indentured servitude even if she did give him a very slim cut of the profits. Shay was good about rewarding effort.

But directing his talent toward helping the tomb raider had pushed him into areas he'd never imagined.

Areas such as Project Nephilim, whose files proved that not only did the government know about non-Oriceran extra-terrestrials, they'd recovered their artifacts.

"If you've got a little stone with an alien language, you've probably got an alien ship stowed somewhere. I just *know* it."

Peyton's fingers flew across the keyboard. He'd been stopped early when he'd hacked the Department of Defense systems and recovered the initial records on the alien research project, but that didn't mean the government was guarding everything as competently. Now that he knew what he was looking for, it was far easier to snoop around the net.

A window popped up on his screen.

"Now Homeland Security, huh? Let's see what you've got for me." A document popped up. "What the hell?" He rushed out of the office.

The door to the Fiat was open, and Shay was halfway in.

"Wait," Peyton shouted.

Shay stood and eyed him. "I don't really have time to wait around for pizza experiments if that's what this is about. I've got to pick up Lily and get her back here and then go talk to someone at the university about the symbols on Brownstone's necklace."

Peyton chuckled. "Although my pizza experiments

redefine the glory of what could be called pizza, this isn't about that."

"What then?"

"I was poking around, and I just found out we have some competition."

Shay shrugged. "We've got a lot of competition. Tomb raiding's not exactly a forgiving business."

Peyton shook his head. "I'm not talking about that. I'm talking about on the alien stuff."

"Oh, don't worry about it. If you found something, I'm sure it's just that Correk guy looking into it on the other end for his Elf Mafia buddies or whoever." She frowned. "That reminds me, I need to check into that guy more."

"I don't think Correk would go to the Professor to hire you, then go to the government to hire an outside contractor."

Shay frowned. "Outside contractor?"

"Yeah. I haven't found a lot of details, just that the Department of Homeland Security is paying a 'retrieval specialist' a shit-ton of money to look into any artifacts related to Project Nephilim. Departments of Energy and Defense are kicking in, too."

"An outside contractor versus creepy government guys?" She frowned. "It smells like they hired a tomb raider."

Peyton sighed. "That's what I was thinking. Maybe all this stuff isn't worth looking into. There might be too much heat."

"Bullshit. First, I want to know the truth about all this crap. We're on the edge of verifying historical information that is considered fringe if not laughable in the academic community. Second, there's money to be made, just like with the Lake Michigan stone."

"You plan to sell the stuff if you find it?"

"Maybe. Got to find it first. With this Brownstone assassin-and-Harriken shit I don't want to take off too soon, but at least we can do background checks. What about the retrieval specialist? Any info? Name?"

Peyton shook his head. "Not yet. The only thing I've found is the payment information."

Shay slipped into her car. "Keep at it then. And, just to be clear, I also still want you to find me a good job. The way Brownstone rolls, this latest Harriken shit won't last longer than a week or two."

Shay pulled out of the parking lot and onto the street. Her meeting with Professor Armstrong at the university only reinforced a startling truth that was threading her Brownstone and alien research together.

The symbols on Brownstone's amulet didn't match the symbols on the alien stones, but she could no longer ignore the obvious. Brownstone's amulet was of non-Oriceran extraterrestrial origin.

She took a deep breath as she turned onto the highway. Several puzzle pieces were falling into place. Brownstone had gated from another world, except it wasn't Oriceran. Some aspects of his background now made more sense. He'd told her that he'd been tested, including magically, and it had been confirmed that he wasn't from Oriceran.

But you can only find what you're testing for, and no one

would even think to test if he's alien. And if his amulet changes his DNA somehow, they might not have been able to figure it out that way.

Shay frowned. The only thing she couldn't determine was if that meant Brownstone's amulet had any relationship to the alien stones. She found it hard to believe there were two lost alien worlds that most people didn't know about.

The tomb raider laughed. Twenty years ago most people hadn't known about Oriceran, and until recently she hadn't even known about any other planets with intelligent life. On second thought, it wasn't so strange that there might be more than one alien world out there.

"I've got to get to the bottom of this shit, but what the hell am I supposed to tell Brownstone?"

She could put it off for a while. Add it to the list of things she was keeping to herself… like Lily.

Brownstone had more immediate concerns. One way or another they'd need to handle the assassins soon, and she suspected his troubles would only end if they snuffed it out at the source in Japan.

Time to take a trip. Peyton would have to babysit Lily. Maybe that was the other way around.

It was a rare clear sky over Los Angeles as Shay drove into Warehouse Two, exhausted after the world's bloodiest and most thrilling vacation.

It wasn't a huge surprise, but worrying about killing high-end assassins and helping Brownstone murder hundreds of Harriken had cut into her research time. The days had blurred together, starting with an ambush at LAX where they'd killed the first assassin, and then the trip to Japan where they'd finished the rest of the assassins and the Harriken.

All the bloodletting and massacres had given her some important tips. First, Shay was still good at her old job, and second, the shadow of her past lurked closer than she realized, courtesy of her encounter with one of the assassins, a Japanese woman, Hisa. The memory lingered in her thoughts.

Shay whipped out a knife and stabbed Hisa in the back. "He's not disrespecting you, bitch. He's respecting me."

The assassin collapsed to the ground, coughing blood. She turned her head, her eyes wide, to stare up at Shay. "No, it can't be! You're dead!"

"Yeah, I'm dead," Shay murmured to herself as she stepped out of her car.

She'd changed her hair color when she'd left her old life behind, but she hadn't gone through the trouble of plastic surgery or magic to alter her appearance. Stubbornness, some might say. Or stupidity.

Lily stepped around the corner. She was holding a cheese sandwich. "Oh, didn't know you were coming in today."

Shay shrugged, taking a long look at the girl, wondering what she wasn't saying. "What am I gonna do, sit at home?"

Peyton came around the corner with his own sandwich, dressed in breeches and laughed. "It wouldn't hurt to take a little while off after helping end an entire international criminal gang."

"Screw that. I'm ready to stop with the whole helping-Brownstone-for-free thing and go back to making money."

"Well, I've got a line on something in Australia. Just checking the background still."

"I helped him ferret out the background." Lily flounced down on the couch.

"Shouldn't you be hanging out with friends or something?"

"Friends around here are overrated. What would I do with them? Talk about buying shoes and boys and summer plans? Or how about the best gun to take as a backup and how to defeat an Ice bitch." Lily's lip curled as she mentioned the witch.

"We have to find you another girlfriend besides Peyton."

"Hardy har." Peyton took a large bite of his sandwich. "Someone had to add some feminine energy in here, besides Lily."

Shay arched an eyebrow at him and waved a hand. "Will it be ready by tomorrow?"

"Probably." Peyton took another bite of his sandwich and stared at her.

"What? Something on my face?"

"This is what I mean. You're not an easy sharer. How it'd go?"

Shay shrugged. "You know how it went. We came, we saw, we massacred."

He walked into the office to place what was left of his sandwich on a plate on the desk. "Not talking about that.

I'm talking, you know, personal stuff. I meant what I said about having your back in that sort of thing."

The tomb raider grimaced. She'd almost put the conversation out of her mind, which had been easy enough with the busy days in Japan.

"Look, um… He understands now that I'm interested in more than just a partnership on jobs." She shrugged, glancing over at Lily, wondering if she was venturing into TMI.

"You don't have to edit yourself around me. There wasn't a lot of privacy in that nuclear escape tunnel. Not a lot I haven't already seen."

Shay cringed, wondering yet again if she was doing right by the teenager.

"I already know that look and for the hundredth time, no to the school of hormonal magic. I'm not going," said Lily, her leg draped over the arm of the couch. "Back to you. Peyton already told me everything anyway."

Shay scowled at Peyton. "I thought you were better than that at keeping secrets."

"I'm selectively brilliant at it."

"Not much to say. Neither one of us is running around sleeping with other people, but we're together."

Peyton shook his head. "Yet you still call the man 'Brownstone.'"

"It's his fucking name isn't it?"

The man offered a placating gesture. "Okay, okay, but did you tell him about the alien stuff?"

"Yeah. Don't think he buys it entirely, but I told him about his amulet."

"What about the other stuff? The government stuff?"

"Nope. Not gonna."

"Really?

Shay nodded. "Look, the guy likes everything simple as possible, and is already OCD because of how he was raised, or maybe that's just how they are on his home planet of Interior Decoratis IV or whatever. I don't know. One interesting clue. He's not Oriceran."

"Then what is he?" asked Lily.

"To be determined, I think. The last thing he needs is to obsess over is the other alien shit if we're not even sure it's connected."

"You don't think it'll be dangerous? That someone might come after him?" asked Peyton, sitting down at his computer.

She burst out laughing. "Who? The government? Given what Brownstone has done to the Harriken, even *if* the government figured out he was an alien, there's no fucking way they'd risk coming after him. You're the one who said he'd win against a country."

"Good point."

"Wow, not Oriceran, not from Earth… maybe." Lily let out a low whistle.

Shay let out another chuckle. "Nah. We'll keep looking into the other angle. If something comes up that he needs to know about, I'll tell him." The mirth vanished from her face, and she glared at Peyton. "And that means you don't tell him, either. Understand?"

"Sure, sure. And same goes for our junior tomb raider."

"Shay's not worried about me." Lily sat up on the edge of the couch, restless and stood up, jumping neatly backward till she was standing on the couch. She leapt to a nearby chair and out the door, onto the top of the closet cubicle square. She kept going, moving further away from them, traveling the warehouse without hitting the floor.

"She does that a lot these days," said Peyton, shrugging his shoulders. "You get used to it after a while. I think she's bored. Teenagers. Set her lose in a mall already."

"I picture her perched on a railing somewhere stalking something. This will have to be a problem for another day. In the meantime, you don't tell Brownstone about what we find *or* about Lily. Capiche?"

"Don't worry about it. Got to finish checking into the Australia job anyway."

Shay gave him a curt nod and sighed. Brownstone liked his life simple, but hers was getting more complicated by the second.

Australia would help. All her running around investigating aliens and killing gangsters had messed with her head, not to mention opening her up to Brownstone. She was drifting from her original plan, and it was time to return to the path with a tomb raid where she could deal with normal threats—just mundane everyday annoyances like Ice Witches and ghosts.

3

Shay stared down at the piles of weapons, knives, and other supplies on the tables in Warehouse Three. Peyton had called and told her to meet him at that location. He apparently believed she'd be ready to head out the minute he explained the job.

"Missing a little something?" Shay inquired.

Peyton looked offended. "Like what?"

"Lily for one." She pointed at him. "Fashion sense, a close second." His current combination of madras shorts and a Wham T-shirt was killing her. Apparently, it was Casual Day at the office.

"Girls dig this look."

"That look gets you girls?" Shay shook her head. "Blind girls, maybe."

Peyton averted his eyes. "Well, a certain kind of girls. You know, confused ones with daddy issues."

"Oh, strippers."

The man groaned and shrugged. "Lily is probably

hanging from the rafters. Give her a second, she'll make a grand entrance. I'm surprised she hasn't begged you to go on the mission."

"I noticed that too. I'm not going to beg for trouble, just this once."

"And instead leave trouble here with the Chameleon."

"Don't do that." Shay grinned. "But I was really talking about the lack of serious electronics in the equipment loadout."

"Ah, that." Peyton shook his head. "The Chameleon doesn't forget."

Shay rolled her eyes. "I swear I'll pull my gun on you if you talk like that again."

"You're no fun, you know that? Anyway, the lack of electronics is a feature, not a bug. That's why I wanted you to come here instead of wasting time doing the briefing at Warehouse Two."

Shay crossed her arms. "Okay, get down to it."

"I've cross-checked the client, and he's offering a million per artifact for the recovery of three different artifacts."

"That sounds like a lot of work."

Peyton shook his head. "The good news is all those artifacts should be at the same site in Australia."

"Australia isn't exactly small." Shay gestured for him to continue.

"You ever hear of the Mahogany Ship?"

"Yep. They say that before Captain Cook or even the Dutch sightings, an earlier ship made landfall in Australia."

Peyton nodded eagerly. "That's the executive summary. From what I've been able to find, it was Portuguese. Our client has provided a map and some information to get you to the ship."

"If it's so easy, why does he need a tomb raider?"

"Because it's in a weird part of the Outback. Even the aborigines have avoided it for centuries. They claimed the area was cursed, but mostly it seems to have some sort of weird energy field that disrupts electronics and even messes with non-electronic compasses. Also, there are more than a few legends about nasty monsters, and...a few sightings that are a lot more recent. I'm not talking poisonous snakes, but things like drop bears."

Shay searched her memory, but the name didn't ring a bell. "'Drop bears?'"

"Basically, think giant carnivorous koala bears that jump down from trees to maul you."

"Great, and the Aussies aren't cleaning this shit up?"

Peyton shrugged. "The monsters stay in the cursed area, and it's in the middle of a desert in the center of the country, and small, relatively speaking. With all the trouble with electronics, I guess they figure it's just not worth the trouble."

Shay rubbed the bridge of her nose. "Wait, so I'm not going to be able to drive around? This will take fucking forever."

"Can you ride a horse?"

"I'm not an equestrienne, but I can manage."

Lily sprinted up to the doorway of the office. "You can handle it."

Peyton eyed her, looking her up and down. "Look who's being super supportive. Where have you been hiding?"

Shay watched Lily keep a faint smile on her face. That

girl is hiding something. No time to dig it out of her. That would take days, if then.

"Lily's right. I can handle it."

Peyton gave a shrug and clapped his hands together. "Then it'll work out perfectly. They might have trouble flying or driving in the area, but it shows up on satellite well enough. At least the terrain. Not so much the ship."

"Maybe the ship isn't there?"

"Nope. It's just, there's weird distortion in the images. The client insists it's there."

"How am I supposed to navigate in the middle of the desert without any of my electronics?"

Peyton smiled. "I've got a course plotted for you from oasis to oasis." He rubbed his hands, an eager gleam in his eye. "I've got it all printed up. Old-school maps, none of this fancy tech stuff."

"Says the man who pretty much lives behind a computer," said Shay.

He put a hand up to the side of his mouth and whispered to Lily. "This is how the grownups got around back when CDs were all the rage. Had to look down while driving."

"What's a CD?"

"Exactly."

He shrugged. "I'm the research assistant and handsome, stylish hacker. Not the tomb raider."

Shay scoffed. "Explain one thing to me."

"What?"

"How does a Portuguese ship end up in the middle of the desert?"

Peyton grinned. "Because the crew were rude."

"I'm rude all the time, and I... Well, LA *is* pretty arid." She shrugged.

"Not arguing, but you weren't some new asshole showing up and screwing with a local and powerful... Well, I guess we'd call him a wizard or something like that, but the aboriginal dude they pissed off had serious magic."

"Strong enough artifact would do it. Those things are like magical storage facilities. What? I grew up around magic. Trifling magic, but still." Lily played with a long lock of grey hair. Somehow, on her it only made her look younger.

"Look who's making a contribution. Now I know something's up."

Shay glared at Peyton to get him back on track and off Lily. She had only known the teenager a short time but the girl clammed up even tighter when cornered.

"Fine," said Peyton. "Where there's a will there's a way. He teleported the entire damned ship into the center of the country to punish the Portuguese for killing some of the locals, and they died. A lot of that stuff was covered up until the truth of Oriceran came out."

Shay shook her head. "If they all died in the middle of the desert, how does anyone even know about them?"

"The captain was a wizard. He wasn't as strong as the guy he screwed with, but he had a few toys at his disposal." Peyton held up a finger. "Artifact number one, a magic quill made from a raven's feather. You dip it in magic ink and write on a special piece of paper, and the message appears in another place, far away.

"Our client recovered a copy of some of the communications between that wizard and his boss in Lisbon, and that's how we know the details." He held up a second finger. "There's a magic compass that you can adjust to track different things. Like instead of pointing north, it can point toward the nearest land."

"I have that. It's called GPS."

"Sure, but it was cool back in the day." Peyton shrugged. "And he's still willing to pay a million for it."

"A million dollars," whispered Lily, her eyes widening.

"Junior Tomb Raider, that's a small job."

"What else?" Shay was tempted to reach out and thump Peyton to keep him on track.

He held up a third finger. "A lantern that uses oil, but somehow doesn't use it up."

"It's an eternal lantern?"

"Yeah, basically."

Shay furrowed her brow. "Pretty low-key when you think about it. I'm used to these guys wanting some ridiculous zombie rod or shit like that."

Lily took a step back and bent backward into a handstand, balancing easily on her fingertips, still talking. "That's something I've never seen before. Zombies were supposed to be a myth."

Peyton leaned down to talk to her. "Not a myth."

Shay watched how easily Lily was moving. It was as if she had to keep moving to work off some of the energy. All the training was making her even more graceful and athletic. Look out Ice Witch. Shay felt a shudder pass down her spine and made herself snap back to the present.

She was glad she was hitting the road on another mission. Stop thinking about Brownstone, a hormonal moody magical teenager and a partner who was brilliant and a loose cannon all at once.

"I looked into the client," Peyton said. "The guy's been trying to get people to do the job for cheaper, but no one would go into the cursed lands for what he was offering. Also, several previous expeditions have ended up...not coming back."

"And you don't have the location from the satellite images? No patterns in the distortion?"

Peyton shook his head. "We have the terrain, but not the ship. I've combed through the research, and I've located some likely spots from surviving eyewitness accounts. The place has always been dangerous, but it wasn't *quite* as dangerous before."

Shay groaned. "It might not even be there. Are you fucking *kidding* me?"

"He's willing to pay ten percent down just for you to try."

"Really? Guess it's time for a little walkabout then."

Shay took note. Not once did Lily ask to go. Yeah, something was definitely up. She reminded herself that the teenager had survived just fine on her own till recently. She would let Shay in when she was ready, and Shay would hope that was soon enough.

Shay's horse clopped along, and she smiled at the pleasant breeze. Back in the States spring was close to giving way to summer, but the magic of hemispheres provided a more tolerable autumn vibe and even a few clouds as she rode through the sparsely vegetated red sand and dirt of the Outback. Red-orange sandstone outcroppings rose from the land to break up the monotony. She wouldn't want to live there, but the sweeping vistas provided a nice bonus.

She pulled out her satellite phone. *Useless.* It wasn't just a crap signal. It wouldn't even turn on. She'd brought an external power supply to try and beat the strange energy-sapping field, but it didn't help.

The scariest thing about a cursed desert for a modern person is that it kills their phones.

No vehicle, no phone, and a lot of slow travel. Her horse was reliable enough, but she had remembered why she didn't like riding horses. For all their majesty and beauty, they were crap factories. Getting used to the smell was taking some time.

Shay chuckled. "At least I'm not riding *behind* anyone."

She fished her map out of her backpack. Without even a normal compass, she needed to be careful. She might not have been some circa 1750 Royal Navy sailor, but she knew enough about following the direction of the sun and Southern Cross to get her going in what should generally be the right direction.

The detailed topographical map also provided several useful landmarks to guide her travel. If she were zooming along in a truck, it might be more of an issue, but the casual pace of the horse gave her plenty of time to adjust.

There was nothing to do but settle in for a couple of days of riding to the potential sites of the Mahogany Ship.

A woman could lose herself in a desert landscape after a while. Shay already had. All the sandstone outcroppings had started to look the same. The shrubs weren't impressive, and the birds flying overhead and scurrying lizards were just annoying. The few trees she spotted, mostly gum, were spindly and distant, as if mocking her.

The monotony of the trip wore at her. There were no distractions. No phone, no internet, no one else to talk to. Nothing but the land and Shay, alone with her thoughts. And that was the last place she wanted to be. This trip was supposed to take her away from all the buzzing in her brain.

Things were easier when she was a killer. Almost all her targets had been in cities or towns. She was never far from civilization, or at least a distraction, for more than a short period.

Her new job wasn't that much different. Normally rural locations weren't so far away in an age of technology and magic, and most of her targets hadn't required lengthy time commitments. Even during most tomb raids in rural areas she could read or listen to material on her phone, but this cursed desert forced her into an important realization.

"Damn, I'm such a fucking city girl." Shay laughed and patted the horse. "I wonder what Brownstone would do if he were out here, a thousand miles away from any barbeque."

She'd taken to talking to herself and the horse on the second day of travel. A human voice soothed, even her own.

The horse swished its tail, whether in response or not, Shay wasn't sure. Some sort of talking Oriceran horse would have been nice, but she wasn't sure if such an animal existed.

"I'm allegedly dating the guy now, but I still don't understand him," Shay mumbled to herself. "I just don't fucking get him. He's not gay and we're together, so…" She laughed. "Fuck, I wonder if the guy is a virgin? I didn't even think of the possibility. I guess I shouldn't press him. He'll make a move when he's ready."

The horse nickered.

"Oh, you agree? What do you know, you're just a horse. You're not dating an alien badass with the social savvy of a turnip. He's a badass though. First man I've ever met who can keep up with me."

The horse neighed.

"Yeah, I agree with whatever you said. Go find an alien horse, and you'll be all hooked up."

Just a few more hours to the first site marked on her map.

"Son of a bitch," Shay growled.

As if the desert were mocking her even more, there were almost no plants, and no rock formations or plateaus for miles. Australia wanted to be very clear to her that there was no teleported shipwreck at the first search point.

"Whatever. Got a few more sites to check."

Shay's horse neighed and shook his head.

"What's your problem? It's not like we even have to stop for you to do your business."

A loud bellow shattered the calm.

Shay spun her head toward the source. A large, dark shape was charging toward them. She pulled on the reins to turn the horse.

"Fuck, what now?"

Whatever it was, it was coming at her from the direction of the next oasis.

Shay kicked the horse into a gallop, which he was more than happy to provide. If they could lose the creature, they could circle back toward the oasis before hitting the next possible ship site.

The horse kicked up dust as it charged through the few shrubs in the area. The dark shape closed on the horse. It was damned fast.

The tomb raider kept a hand on the reins as she pulled out her 9mm. She wouldn't need any electricity to blast a few rounds behind her.

Her horse whinnied, terror propelling it forward. Shay spared another glance behind her. Their pursuer had closed to about thirty yards.

"What the fuck? I think I preferred those frog assholes in Russia."

The creature lumbered toward her on six thick legs. Although it was hard to tell from a distance, it looked like it had a foot or two on Shay's horse's length. Two bulbous black eyes topped its squat reddish face, and a mixture of scales and patchy fur covered the rough hide.

Okay, not a drop bear. Maybe a bunyip? Yeah, that was it. They allegedly liked water, and it had come from the direction of the oasis.

Shay squeezed off a few rounds at the bunyip, but it

didn't even bother to stagger. Her horse neighed but didn't buck.

"Guess it's a good thing I asked for a horse used to gunfire," she muttered. She was officially in Australia on a "hunting" trip.

The bunyip closed to twenty yards. Four more rounds didn't do much more than her first shots.

Shay holstered her pistol. There was no point in wasting ammunition. Her gaze dropped to the wrapped sheath of the *tachi* lashed to the saddlebags. The tomb raider reached back to grab the *tachi*.

The bunyip bellowed again, and pain blasted through Shay's head and her vision darkened. Several long moments passed before she could focus. Her horse lay on the ground, twitching but not bleeding. She was also on the ground, her hands and face scraped and her sword a few feet away.

What the fuck? Some sort of sonic attack? I'm lucky I didn't break my neck.

The monster approached, this time at a leisurely pace. Its open mouth revealed a row of twitching sucker-covered appendages surrounding a circle of needle-like fangs.

Shay shook her head to try to clear it and pushed herself to her feet, although her stomach was lurching and the world was still spinning around her. The bunyip's cry had gone well beyond simply intimidating prey.

The tomb raider stumbled and fell to her knees in front of the *tachi*. She reached out to snatch up the blade with a shaking hand.

"You sure are an ugly son of a bitch."

Shay forced herself up again and gripped the sword

tightly with both hands. The monstrosity charged her, but she held her ground.

Five yards. Four. Three.

Stomach churning and the horizon still rocking, Shay spun to the side and slashed with the *tachi*. The magical weapon dug deeply into the monster. It roared as green blood sprayed from the wounds and tumbled to the ground.

Shay stumbled toward it and kept stabbing into the monster's head until it stopped moving.

The tomb raider stood there for a long moment, her sword covered in the blood of a legendary beast and her lunch threatening to come up.

She shuffled over to her horse. The animal whinnied and pushed to its feet.

Shay took the reins, grateful that he hadn't immediately bolted and apparently didn't have any broken bones.

"Hey, I know we're both unsteady. How about I just walk with you a while?"

They walked forty feet before Shay looked back at the dead bunyip.

"By the way, I hope you're fucking endangered, asshole."

4

―――――――――

Shay let out a yelp of joy and the horse nickered.

The setting sun painted the sky an orange-red, highlighting the angular shape of the ship half-buried in the red sand, its prow pointing upward as if it were ready to launch into the sky.

A massive gum tree stood next to the ship. Since it was one of the few large ones she'd spotted since entering the cursed lands, and with no obvious water sources nearby, she assumed the wizard had helped the tree grow with magic.

Shay pulled out her pistol and pointed it upward as she scanned the tree. There was no way she was letting some drop bear ambush her, but there wasn't a single animal in the branches, magical or otherwise.

She holstered her pistol and returned her attention to the Mahogany Ship. The masts were missing, with evidence of cuts centuries ago suggesting a purposeful removal. There was no sign of the sails or much of anything on the top deck. The colorful sand of the central Australian desert had infiltrated the ship through its many cracks and holes, but the wreck was well-preserved otherwise. That was likely due to the dry conditions or a spell, or maybe both.

The tomb raider didn't care much about the reason. She only cared that she'd found it.

Of course, the damned Mahogany Ship had to be at the last site she'd checked, but it didn't matter now. She'd found the cursed thing, and soon she could get the hell out of the desert and away from all the bizarre and violent creatures inhabiting the area.

The trip could have merely been annoying with a little violent spice from the bunyip, but that was only the start of her fun. She'd had to take down two more bunyips, some giant lizard bigger than a Komodo dragon, and some sort of weird-ass tentacle that popped out of the sand. Given the size of the last, she didn't even want to think about the body of the creature it had been attached to.

Her solution had been to flee. Being brave when it could get you killed was just another way of being an idiot.

"You thought *you* had problems, Brownstone. All you had were some gangsters trying to kill you. This entire fucking *country* is trying to kill me! The Australians should just get someone to nuke this place for them."

Shay shook her head. He would never know about her troubles. She couldn't tell him.

The man might be a badass, but he didn't deal with the kind of shit she did, at least not on a regular basis. He'd killed a strange creature in Japan, but for the most part, Brownstone stuck to two-legged threats. The last thing she needed was for him to tag along on every job out of worry.

Sometimes absence really *did* make the heart grow fonder.

She dismounted and tied her reins to the gum tree before she made her way to the ship, sword in hand. With her luck on this trip, there was probably a zombie kangaroo waiting inside to rip her throat out.

Shay sheathed her blade and scampered up the side of the ship where the hull met the ground. The mild angling of the bow made climbing onto the deck a challenge more of concentration than true agility. With careful steps, she made her way toward the captain's quarters. The door collapsed with a thud at her touch, the hinges long ago rusted into oblivion.

According to the client's records, the rest of the crew had attempted to flee into the desert, which might explain the absence of the masts. They must have tried to use the wood somehow.

The wizard had stayed behind, trusting his superiors to recover him and unable to admit his magic to the mundane crew.

Shay shook her head. The light illuminated a skeleton in a chair against the back wall of the room, which was pinned by a desk. Holes and cracks in the floor revealed that the desk had once been bolted down, but time and gravity had won against Portuguese carpentry and metal-working.

The skeleton's head was slumped forward. There was a

flintlock pistol in his right hand and a lead ball embedded in the skull.

Shay sucked in a breath. "Guess I wouldn't have waited to starve, either. Sorry, pal."

His tattered uniform was more scraps of fabric than proper clothing at that point, but the fact that there was anything left after centuries was impressive.

Something glinted in the skeleton's other hand. Shay stepped forward to peer closer. *The compass.*

"Sorry, but it's not like you need it anymore."

Shay extracted it and dusted off the fine layer of sand covering the silver. If she had any doubts about its magical nature, the lack of tarnish on a centuries-old silver compass dispelled them.

A quick shove repositioned the desk, then she grabbed a drawer and pulled, but the handle snapped off after an inch.

Shay shook her head and pulled out the drawer from the top. There was nothing in there but dust and the hint of something that might have been paper long ago. The second drawer contained a few lead balls.

"Come *on.*"

The tomb raider knelt and inspected the final drawer, which held a black feather quill.

"Now we're talking. Just need the lantern, and I'm out of here."

Shay grinned. She wouldn't say it was the easiest three million she'd ever earned, but she was satisfied with the job. She looked around the cabin, and her smile faded.

There was no lantern in the captain's cabin.

She scrubbed a hand over her face.

"I'm really gonna have to check this whole ship?"

The tomb raider shook her fist. "Seriously, Australia? Why do you hate me?"

It had taken Lily an hour to come up with an excuse that got her out of Warehouse Two and out from under Peyton's curious eye.

She tried saying she wanted to go get a burger. but he offered to drive. When she changed her mind and said she was going to work out first, maybe she'd run the distance between the two warehouses, Peyton only grew more suspicious, peppering her with questions.

"You're meeting someone. Is it a guy? I'd understand. You're a teenager," he had said.

She stared at him, working on a different storyline that would get him to back off when it hit her.

"I need to get some, uh… girl things." She kept the stare going, daring him to look away.

Peyton slowly turned red and sputtered, even throwing some of the petty cash at her.

That'll teach him. Lily smiled as she got on the crosstown bus to Wilshire Boulevard. She didn't want to tell him, tell anyone that she was going to the nuclear escape tunnel. Going home.

Lily slipped behind the strip mall and rows of green metal dumpsters to a hidden door between two of the stores. It looked like it had to be a second entrance to one of the stores and once opened, a curious passerby would have been met with a large steel door locked tight.

Lily grabbed hold of the handle and felt a lurch through her body. The tumblers in the lock fell into place and she pulled back, using her weight to get the door open just wide enough to slip through. The heavy backpack on her back just barely fitting. Weird magic.

She stepped off the short platform and felt nothing but air, reaching out for the metal ladder she knew was there.

She scrambled down the ladder, whistling out the old signal that it was her, not knowing if the code had changed and everyone would scatter.

By the time she made her way down the ladder and worked through the tunnels to the camp she found no one there. Her heart dropped from the disappointment.

She let out another loud, low whistle and waited to hear anything in return. Nothing. One more time.

Finally, she heard splashing and the sound of someone running toward her. She pressed back against the cement wall, not sure who was coming yet. No one had answered with the end of the code.

A tall, thin teenage boy with rumpled brown hair emerged from one of the tunnels.

"Harry!" Lily ran toward him with relief and hugged him tight around his neck. "I thought you were all gone."

Harry hugged her back and could feel the newly defined muscles in her arms. He stood back from her to get a better look. "You thought we were gone? I pretty much wrote you off. How long has it been? Who was that woman? What happened to you?"

"That's a lot of questions, Harry. Not even sure I can answer them all. Where is everybody else? I brought food and some clothes. They're a little unusual. I kind of borrowed them from a friend of mine."

"Everyone is at the new encampment. You know us, we move around every week or so, just in case. You come back to stay?"

Lily looked down for a moment and squeezed her eyes shut, not sure what to say. "No, not this time. It's just a visit." She offered him the bag. "I can't stay too long."

"You got yourself a home, Lily. That's a good thing."

"This is home, Harry. I'm going back because I'm learning a trade. Tomb raider. I even saw the Ice bitch again." Lily shook her head. "And I lost again, but each time I learn a little more about her. Her end of days is coming."

Harry took her hand. "Be careful out there. We'll be here when you're ready to come back."

"I'll stop by again when I can slip away without anyone seeing me."

Harry backed up in the direction he came and tilted his head back, letting out a loud bird call that echoed through the pipes. He smiled as the sound of running feet echoed and filled the pipes with sound.

Lily's eyes filled with tears as she waited. He had let out the distress call that anyone living underground would answer, no matter what. One by one they came into view and saw her standing there, even as they swiveled around looking for trouble.

Petie, a young wizard noticed the smile on Harry's face

and caught on first, rushing at Lily to hug her. Everyone else quickly followed, patting her on the head and squeezing her till she thought she would pass out. She loved it all. Family.

"I'll be back, I swear."

Shay muttered to herself as she set up her sleeping bag in the desert. The damned lantern hadn't been anywhere on the ship, and now she was left with nothing but exhausted muscles and the bright moon hanging in the sky as if taunting her.

She shrugged at her sleeping horse.

"How the hell am I supposed to find a lantern that could be, uh, *anywhere* in Australia?"

Shay laid her sheathed sword and tactical harness beside the sleeping bag. The lantern would have to wait. She could light her own non-eternal lantern, but right now her muscles ached and fatigue fogged her mind.

The horse'd had the right idea. It was time for some sleep. She unzipped her sleeping bag.

Something flickered in the distance.

"What the fuck was that?"

Shay narrowed her eyes. More flickers.

"What now? Some Australia firefly that's five feet long and has acid breath?"

The tomb raider rolled her eyes and grabbed binoculars from her saddlebags. Shay laughed as she looked through them.

"That's about the last thing I expected, but it's almost a relief."

Six men on horseback rode in her direction, a couple carrying lanterns. Their holsters at their sides cleared up the question if they were armed, but not if they were a danger to her. Only an idiot would have wandered these cursed desert lands without weapons, but the kind of men who were prepared to face such dangers were often the same kind who'd kill people rather than walk away.

Shay slipped her tactical harness back on but left the sword on the ground. A gun and her knives would be sufficient to deal with humans. She jogged over to the gum tree, where she could maintain line-of-sight on the new arrivals but still retain some cover.

The tense minutes passed as the men rode closer. In the moonlight she'd be harder to spot than they were with their lanterns, but she wasn't invisible, which explained why they slowed as they neared the site.

"Just turn around and leave," Shay called. "You're too late."

One of the men raised a hand, and all of them brought their horses to a stop.

"Now *this* was about the last thing I expected," the man called back. His accent was American.

"The site's been looted. Nothing here for you."

"By you?"

"The point is, there's nothing left."

The man sighed and shook his head. "Sorry. We can't walk away from this. Do you have any idea how many creatures attacked us on our way here?"

"Yeah, I'm sure it's been a big fucking pain. Not exactly like it's been Easy Street for me."

Several of the men's hands rested near their pistol grips, and Shay's hand drifted toward her holster. The red sand was about to get even redder.

"I've got to say, though," the man continued, "I'm impressed. When I heard about the great Aletheia taking the job, I thought there was no way a single tomb raider would be insane enough to go into the middle of the cursed desert by herself when she couldn't even call for extraction if things got too hot."

Shay's jaw tightened. These men shouldn't have known she was involved, even through her alias. The fact they did and were still there wasn't a good sign.

"What can I say? I'm a crazy bitch, but I'm not walking away."

"Because of Antarctica?"

Fucking Yulia.

Shay narrowed her eyes. "Because I complete my jobs."

The men all laughed before their leader spoke again. "I've got nothing but respect for you. You came onto our scene like a lightning bolt. It wasn't all that long ago that no one had heard of you, but you've pounded out high-profile raids left and right by yourself." He sighed. "That still doesn't mean I can let you have the artifacts. Here, I'll even cut you a deal—one we can all be happy about."

"A deal?"

"Yeah. Ride back with us, and we'll split the proceeds. Fair's fair. We're all taking a hit, but then no one has to worry about getting shot."

Shay shook her head.

"Well, the other option is we just shoot you and leave your body here for the buzzards, but fuck...there aren't even many buzzards around this place. Live hard, die young, and leave a good-looking corpse and all that." The man shrugged and grinned. "I know you're supposed to be tough, but, sorry, honey, we outnumber you six to—"

Shay's shot punched the man off his horse. His horse reared, and several of the nearby horses did as well. The tomb raider took advantage of the confusion to keep shooting. Three of the men fell before the group managed to counterattack, and the poor bastard who'd managed to get the shot off received a 9mm bullet in his chest for his trouble.

The whole fight, if Shay could even call the one-sided slaughter that, was over in less than thirty seconds. The men's horses rushed in every direction now, some with their riders on the ground, and others dragging dead bodies. Her horse shook its head and whinnied.

"Wait, you seriously just fucking woke up? Talk about a deep sleeper!"

The other horses continued bolting into the darkness. Shay had no idea if the men had somehow been following her, or if they'd just been lucky. The former was unlikely. There weren't a lot of places to hide in the vast expanse of the desert scrubland.

She tsked and shook her head. The only thing the bastards had managed to accomplish was putting a bullet in the gum tree. She felt worse about the hardy tree that had survived centuries in the middle of a cursed wasteland taking a hit than the men she'd killed.

"I gave them the chance to walk away," she murmured to herself.

Shay patted her horse on the shoulder. "Guess we should get away from here, just in case more assholes show up. Sorry, boy. Just a little more riding tonight, then I have to figure out how to track down the last artifact."

The tomb raider shot up at the warm touch of the dawn sun, sore but with a clear mind.

Better than a clear mind. Shay was downright inspired.

She grinned and fished the compass out of the backpack, holding it and concentrating on the eternal lantern.

The tomb raider stifled a huge yawn as she stared down at the silver compass. The background research hadn't provided much information on how to activate the artifacts, so maybe the whole thing was pointless, but it wouldn't hurt to try.

The needle jerked and spun for a few seconds before stopping abruptly. Judging by the sun, it wasn't pointing north.

Shay patted the horse. "I'm so damned smart."

The horse snorted.

"Quiet, you. What are you, a four-legged Peyton?"

A few hours of travel later, Shay stood inside a small cave in a sandstone outcropping staring down at two skeletons with flintlock pistols, swords, and most importantly, a small silver lantern. Tarnish had long since masked its color, but the flickering flame still burned.

Damn, almost five hundred years. That's impressive.

Shay lifted the lantern with a smile. Time to get the hell out of the cursed desert.

5

Shay stretched as she stepped out of her car into Warehouse Two. The mouthwatering smell of freshly-baked pizza hung in the air. She blinked, having not expected it. A large pepperoni pie lay near the pizza oven, cooling.

She slammed the car door and made her way toward the office. It felt like months instead of weeks since she'd last been in the place. After her adventure in Australia, she'd decided to follow up on some ruins in Japan rumored to have alien symbols on them. The trip had been low-key compared to her tomb raid Down Under, with the only real excitement a popped tire.

Peyton emerged from the office with a wave. Today he wore a powder blue double-knit polyester suit, circa the 1970's, but Shay couldn't even work up the energy to make a snarky comment.

Lily was in a white apron, still quiet, working on pulling a pizza out of the oven.

"I've been showing her the ropes." He gestured toward the pizza. "How about a little lunch?"

Shay shrugged and slapped a slice on a paper plate. She sat down in the office and brought the pizza to her mouth. Not the best, but far from bad. She smiled around the bite. So many weeks in the field served as a spice all its own.

"Pretty good," she commented.

Peyton grinned and shrugged. "I'm leveling up. Slowly, but I am."

"Just so you know, I'm only sticking around for a few days. I have some errands to run in South America, concerning Brownstone's amulet and the symbols. I still don't know if his shit is linked to the stones."

Lily looked up suddenly, interested.

The man stared at her. "That's uncanny. You really do have perfect timing."

Shay took another bite of her pizza before bothering to respond. "What the hell are you talking about?"

"I was waiting until you got here to tell you that I've ID'd the retrieval specialist working with Project Nephilim."

"Oh?"

"Francois Durand."

Shay gobbled down the rest of her slice as she processed the information. She frowned and shook her head. "I don't know that name."

Peyton nodded. "I'm not surprised. The guy's almost a ghost. Like you, Gray Ghost."

Lily punched him in the arm, eliciting a short yowl out of him. "Friendly kidding about the truth," protested Peyton.

"Like two people who faked their death?" asked Shay.

"More like a guy who is very, very careful to let only his name get out, nothing else." Peyton pulled out his phone and tapped it for a few moments.

He held it up to display an image of a lean dark-haired man with a jagged scar across the side of his face in a suit. "But when you're as good as I am, you can always grab a picture from a camera somewhere."

Shay nodded, studying the photo in detail. She wanted to recognize the guy instantly if she saw him in a crowd. "What's this guy's deal?"

"Well, he's a French national. Not a big surprise from the name, I know. He's got a good reputation, but not for freelance tomb-raiding work. Mostly organizational contracting stuff. He describes himself as an artifact-retrieval consultant who can be hired for the right price." He pointed toward the picture with his free hand. "That's the good news."

"How?"

"Everything I've ever read about the man suggests he's neutral. Only cares about cash, not politics."

Shay grabbed another slice of pizza. "Doesn't help me if a man screws with me because he's getting paid rather than because he's a true believer. I don't think deep politics are Yulia's motivation."

"She's pure essence of bitch," muttered Lily.

"Just saying that he's not some sort of US Special Forces guy who'll fight you for truth, justice, and apple pie."

"True enough. What's this guy's rep for dealing with interference?"

"I couldn't really find much, just that he's skilled in a

number of relevant areas. Research, firearms...that sort of thing."

"I care more about if he'll try and blow me up with a rocket launcher if he happens to see me near an artifact. If I have to take someone down during a tomb raid because they are going after me I'll do what I have to, but if I'm not careful, Aletheia will end up with a bounty on her head just like Shay Carson." She shrugged. "Guess I'll just have to beat this guy to the artifacts. What else you got? Anything personal?"

Peyton put his phone back in his pocket. "When Durand isn't on a job, he's been spotted around watering holes in DC, London, and Munich."

"But not Paris?"

"Nope."

"Interesting. Has he had any trouble with the French government?"

"Not that I've found, but we'll keep looking. I'm teaching Lily how to hack. We're like Alison's school but instead it's the school of necessary life skills."

"Like online stealing."

Peyton gave Lily a gentle nudge. "I believe we called that lesson, online reappropriation. C minus." He pointed at Shay's pizza. "Eat up before Lily moves on in. The girl can pack it away. You won't be getting seconds if you don't put a move on."

Lily put down the long wooden paddle and slid three pieces onto a paper plate as Peyton nodded in her direction.

Shay was already learning how to let most of their conversations just flow over her, picking out the information she needed and ignoring the rest.

"Keep searching. If there's someone else we can point at this guy to make our lives easier, I'd rather do that." Shay took a bite of her pizza, letting the savory flavors linger on her tongue.

Great. First Yulia, now this guy.

A few days and a visit to South America later, Shay sat at one of the larger tables in Warehouse Four with some books, including several on South and Mesoamerican pyramids and the notes from an expedition to an Egyptian pyramid. The materials had earlier aided her in identifying the alien nature of Brownstone's amulet, and now she wanted to crosscheck the symbols on his amulet against the symbols from the different alien stones.

Photos of the three different stones sat on the table: Mexico, Illinois, and the one from Project Nephilim. A photo of Brownstone's necklace lay right above them, allowing for easy comparison.

Shay was not a linguist, but even she could see the that the symbols on the stone and the symbols on Brownstone's necklace looked nothing alike.

She groaned and rubbed her temples.

Maybe there's no connection there to find? How do I know Brownstone's amulet was made by the same people? Because I just think it sounds too convenient to have two new alien planets? But how the hell can I be sure?

"Guess it's a good thing I didn't become an academic,"

she muttered. "I might have started killing people out of frustration."

Her phone rang. It was Brownstone.

Speak of the alien...

"What's up?" Shay answered.

"What are you doing?"

"Huh?"

"I asked, what are you doing?"

Shay sighed and stared at the pictures. "Research for...a job."

This was the problem with growing closer to the man. Lying to him—even by omission—tightened her stomach, but if Brownstone realized the government might be sniffing around him, it'd end poorly for everyone and a few city blocks would go up in flames.

He was famous enough now from his Harriken antics that the government wouldn't likely make him disappear even if they found out that his amulet was of extraterrestrial origin, and there was no evidence that she or Peyton had stumbled across to suggest that was true anyway. Everything she'd found suggested people assumed Brownstone was just using Oriceran artifacts, and that was if they even knew he possessed superhuman abilities.

"Just was wondering," Brownstone rumbled, snapping Shay out of her thoughts. "We could do some shit together after Mexico."

"I'll...let you know."

"Okay. Talk to you later." He ended the call.

Shay stared at her phone, then set it on the table. Mexico. She'd almost put it out of her mind. The exploration of Brownstone's background in South America had led to conversations in which she'd admitted some of her history and the truth about the men targeting her.

"The Nuevo Gulf Cartel. They were the ones who wanted me dead, but it was more an excuse. It's not like I'm running from them in particular. They make it harder for me, since they'd come after me if they knew I was still alive."

"Aren't you tired of running? Tired of looking over your shoulder?"

Brownstone's go-to solution to the problem of an international criminal gang being after him was to kill people until they stopped, and he'd offered to help her apply it to her problem.

She had to admit there was a certain elegance to the plan of just killing most of your enemies. The cartel had even offered them an opportunity in the form of a leadership meeting, so it was time for a little vacation to Mexico for tequila and murder.

Shay might not be free by the time they were finished, but she was making a whole new set of enemies in her new job, so she might as well clean up some of the old ones.

Peyton winced as he read the phone alert from one of his LAPD monitoring bots.

"Shit, this is bad."

This was supposed to be a great day. After all, the Alien Ass-kicker himself, James Brownstone, was standing in Warehouse Three just around the corner from Peyton. He and Shay were gearing up for their trip to Mexico, so

Peyton was getting a rare opportunity to talk directly with the man.

Shay had conveniently played musical warehouses with Lily, getting Peyton's assistance to move her around one step ahead of Brownstone. Lily grew tired of the game and eventually gave him the slip, not that he was trying that hard to hold on to her.

He knew that when she was determined it was easier to give in. She'd return from one of her mysterious jaunts when she was ready.

Peyton looked back down at the alert on his phone.

Brownstone has all sorts of police contacts. Maybe he has some idea what to do.

Peyton took a few deep breaths and stepped around the corner.

The bounty hunter glanced at him. "Problem, Peyton?"

Guess my face must be telling it all.

"I'm always monitoring stuff in case people are looking for Shay or me." Peyton shrugged.

Brownstone's brow furrowed. "Yeah, and?"

"I was, uh, poking around in the LAPD system, and I found out that AET is looking for Shay."

"Why would AET want Shay? How the hell do they even know who she is?"

"They got a partial image from a drone from that airport fight when you guys took down that assassin before heading to Japan. From what I can tell, the AET reached out and the FBI sent some information back linking the image to...well, Shay. They don't know her real name, but they know she was a hitman on the East Coast and think she's dead, that sort of thing." Peyton sucked in a breath. "Shit, what should we do? If they get serious, it'll be hard for her to hide. Too many drones and cameras in this city."

Brownstone scrubbed a hand over his face. "Keep this to yourself for now."

Peyton's stomach tightened. He'd worked long and hard to earn Shay's trust, and unless he were deluding himself, he'd even earned her friendship. Keeping something like this from her might unravel those bonds.

"You serious? Shay needs to know."

Brownstone shook his head. "You heard me. Shay needs to concentrate on this cartel shit. This AET crap is my fault, because they have such a hard-on for taking me down. Let me handle it. I'll work something out."

Peyton sighed. "You sure? This seems like something I should tell her."

Fuck, fuck, fuck. This is going to end with her pointing a gun at me, I just know it. Is "your boyfriend told me to keep it a secret" a good enough defense with Shay?

"I'll solve the problem," Brownstone rumbled. "For now, Shay needs to be focused. Besides, if I can take down the Harriken and help take down a cartel, I can get a few cops off Shay's ass."

Peyton took a bite of the sausage pizza and frowned. It wasn't bad, but it also wasn't great. Something was still missing—that subtle technique or ingredient that would elevate him from Pizza Pawn to Pizza King.

Still no sign of Lily, but he wasn't going to worry, yet.

Focus on the pizza instead.

He nodded to himself. At least he was close to getting Shay to acknowledge his greatness. For now, he at least had a steady source of lunch and dinner.

Shay's little cartel-cleaning trip with her buff beau had gone well, and the Nuevo Gulf Cartel was a few men away from being a footnote. She'd called him to let him know she had to take down a few guys in Europe and would be back to LA after that.

He rubbed his chin, incidentally removing a bit of sauce.

What the hell am I supposed to do when she gets back? Brownstone still hasn't handled this AET shit. How long am I supposed to keep it from Shay? If she finds out on her own, she'll realize I already knew.

Peyton glanced at the pizza oven. If he could achieve the ultimate pizza, he might be able to distract her enough to avoid a gun to the face.

That's my plan? Survive Shay by the application of pizza?

He grinned. The more he thought about it, the better the plan seemed.

His phone rang, and he grabbed it, assuming it was Shay. He blinked when he spotted Brownstone's number.

Okay, play it cool. Don't mention the pizza plan. Just act like Slick Mercenary Hacker Peyton.

"Hey, are you calling to make me richer?" the researcher answered.

"Shay's still in Europe, right?"

"Yep. Why? Worried?"

"Nah. I just found a solution to the AET shit."

Peyton's heart kicked up. A plan where he didn't have to bake the ultimate pizza was always a good one.

"I'm listening."

"There's a woman sitting in the Leanan Sídhe right now who looks like Shay."

"They say everyone has a twin. Guess you have a type, huh, Brownstone?"

The bounty hunter grunted. "She's a fucking clone. She's wearing one of Shay's dresses and some of her perfume. She's flirting with me like she's never seen a man before. And she's being too nice and calling me James."

Peyton frowned. If Shay had returned from Europe early, she would have at least dropped him a text about it.

"Okay, that's…suspicious and not very Shay."

"Yeah. If AET wants Shay so badly, they can fucking have her twin instead. I don't know who this bitch is, but she's probably not gonna take me out for barbeque, so I figure we get her barbequed instead."

Peyton laughed. "Damn, you're ruthless. What's the plan?"

"Do your computer shit and send an anonymous tip to AET that the killer from NY will be at Lincoln Park in an hour."

"You want AET to go after some strange woman in the middle of a public park?"

"They're cops, they'll clear that shit out. That's why I'm giving them an hour."

Peyton whistled. "You really think this will work?"

"I think AET wants a scalp, so I'm giving them one. Can you do it? And how much will it cost?"

"This is for Shay. It's on the house."

6

Shay stared at Peyton as he stepped out of the Warehouse Two office. Today's sartorial choices included slippers and an ornate Japanese robe decorated with a floral pattern. In another circumstance it might have looked elegant, but not on a man shuffling away from his computer desk with a can of Mountain Dew in his hand.

"Really?" She pointed to his robe. "You know, when I was on the plane, I was entertaining myself by trying to figure out what strange outfit you might wear next. Sometimes you're so close to having a clue, and other times I'm convinced you're snorting all the dust in the county in the morning before choosing your wardrobe."

Peyton shrugged. "This isn't weird. Plenty of Japanese men wear something like this." He sipped his soda.

"Yeah, sure, probably on the weekend in their houses. And in Japan, not at work in a secret warehouse in Los Angeles." Shay gestured around the building.

"We're in a global economy. Well, say what you want, at least it's memorable."

Shay laughed. "You've got me there."

"Exactly. You get to coast by with the femme-fatale thing, but I'm making my mark by being fashion-forward."

"There's such a thing as a man being ahead of his time."

Peyton nodded. "Sure, sure. Anyway, I was trying to get into character. Not a big deal." He set his can down on a nearby table and sighed.

"'Into character?' What, you're trying to get into the mind of some rich new Japanese client or something? This some kind of visualization exercise?"

If that sort of thing motivated his clothing choices, many of them made even less sense than before—or some of their clients were far freakier than she'd realized.

Peyton shook his head. "The Japanese are famous for loyalty and all that." The corners of his mouth pulled up in a smile, and he rubbed his hands together.

Shay didn't like the direction the conversation was going. "And why do you need to get into the mindset of a loyal person?"

"Uh, just, you know, always a good thing. Loyalty, that is." Peyton shrugged.

Fuck. Please don't have screwed me, Peyton. I actually like *you at this point, and I even gave Brownstone a big speech about how the old Shay was dead. Don't bring her back, Mr. Fancy Robe. I almost want to believe what Alison's told me about my soul not looking like a piece of shit.*

She'd already disabled his Deadman's Switch and hadn't received any alerts about him bypassing her efforts. In terms of pure computer skills, Shay would acknowledge, at least to herself, that the man had the edge over her. However, his lack of killer instinct and its accompanying paranoia would always put him at a disadvantage.

Peyton kept rubbing his hands together and looking everywhere but into her eyes. Not a great sign.

Shay shot a smile at the researcher and pulled off her jacket to hang on a hook inside the office. "You look nervous, Peyton."

He swallowed. "I'm not nervous. Why should I be? I've got a beachfront apartment and an awesome cat."

Osiris meowed on cue from the other end of the warehouse. The little furball had gone from lounging around the office to hiding half the time in recent weeks.

Shay slowly pulled her gun out of her holster. She didn't aim it at her assistant, but instead let the hand with the gun hang loosely at her side.

"Where's Lily?" Shay's expression grew dark. "What happened?"

Peyton's gaze dipped to the weapon. "Uh, Shay?"

"Just remembered I need to clean it. It's gotten a lot of use in the last few days. Figured I'd do that while I was here and not running right off to a job."

"Okay. Just to be clear, you're not planning on shooting me, are you?"

Shay took in a long slow breath. "Not unless you give me a reason, so go ahead and spill whatever is eating you. Start with where Lily is."

Peyton's face scrunched, and he groaned. He held up his hands in front of him. "Okay, first, I don't know where Lily is. Don't wave the gun! The kid slips out of here on occasion. She used to bother with excuses, now, she just goes.

Unless I was cleared to duct tape her to a chair that's gonna happen. She's a damn gray elf. I'm not sure the tape would even hold her."

Shay knew Peyton was right. What was she thinking even taking in that girl? She took a quick glance around the warehouse and wondered if it was time to burn the place. "Second thing?" she asked, swinging her attention back to Peyton.

"I guess I'm loyal to a fault, at least to one person at a time."

"What the fuck are you talking about? I'm starting to get confused here, and when I get confused, I get pissed."

"I would have told you earlier, but Brownstone told me not to. It's hard to say no to the Scourge of Harriken, the Granite Ghost, the Alien Ass-kick—"

"Shut it." Shay narrowed her eyes and holstered her weapon. No reason for intimidation now that the man was talking. Well, *babbling*, but it was a form of communication. "Told you to not tell me what?"

"AET was after you. They got a partial image from the LAX fight. Even with your disguise, the FBI was starting to link it to you, at least the old you back in New York. It looked like they were closing in."

"Shit, really?" Shay frowned. "And Brownstone knew? How did you find out? He told *you*, but he didn't tell me? What the fuck is up with that? He barely knows you."

"Uh, it was kind of the other way around."

"How so?"

"I found out about the AET stuff, and I mentioned it to him." Peyton held his hands in front of his chest. "He told me he would handle it. That you needed to concentrate on kicking cartel ass."

Shay shrugged. "I did, kind of, but that doesn't change anything. You're telling me that you had information that police might have identified me and you held it back?"

"I'm sorry. Look, I'm telling you now, even though the Alien Ass-kicker didn't want me to."

"Stop calling him 'the Alien Ass-kicker.'"

Peyton chuckled.

"Anyway, I saved your life. Always remember that."

"You've also threatened it several times."

"Details." Shay went into the office and slumped into a chair. "Fuck. AET? Now I have to figure out how to get them off my ass."

"Oh, don't worry about that. Brownstone already did, and I helped." Peyton stood up taller, a huge grin splitting his face.

"Huh? What the hell did you two do?"

"You see, there was some sort of witch or somebody pretending to be you. She was hitting on Brownstone and he figured out it wasn't you, so he set AET on her with my help." Peyton whistled. "Check out the news. It was a hard-core battle. I don't think Brownstone realized how tough it would be. AET ended up killing her. As far as the LAPD and FBI are concerned you've been killed twice now, and I've poked around in the LAPD systems to confirm it. They aren't looking at you anymore, figuring the body they have is the infamous hitman the FBI was tracking."

Shay crossed her arms. "Let me get this straight... When I was off in Europe finishing off the last few high-level members of the Nuevo Gulf Cartel, you and Brownstone were sitting around conspiring to trick cops into assassinating random witches pretending to be me? Meanwhile, a teenage girl gave you the slip."

Peyton looked to the side for a moment before nodding. "A teenage magical girl, but yeah, that about sums it up. Good news, Brownstone never saw her."

"You're both more ruthless than I realized." Shay snickered. "I kind of like it." She shook her head. "And why was she pretending to be me? Maybe she's some friend of Yulia's."

"Don't know. From what Brownstone said, she was trying to get into his pants. I don't know if it was part of some strategy to get close to him for something else, or if she just wanted a little out-of-this-world bedtime fun."

"Fucking bitch. She's lucky she's dead already." Shay's phone beeped, and she yanked it out of her pocket. She glared down at the alert. "I've got to go. The gnome's back in town." She shot up and snatched her coat from the hook. "By the way, next time you tell *me* first, not Brownstone."

"I'm telling you now."

"Yeah, but next time tell me right away."

Surprise spread across Peyton's face. "Not going to threaten to kill me?"

Shay slipped on her coat. "The fact that you have to look at yourself in the mirror in those outfits is punishment enough. Keep an eye out for Lily, or short of that keep an eye out that she's betrayed us and we need to leave."

Shay took a deep breath and forced her eyes not to slide off the entrance to Prophecy Gaming. Despite all her visits to the shop, it still took all her concentration not to be misled by the glamour defending it.

She maneuvered through the thick mall crowd separating her from the shop and stepped inside. No one manned the front, so she headed directly toward the back room. The door to the back opened before she completed her trip and Tubal-Cain stepped out with a thin smile on his small face.

Shay couldn't tell if he was happy, or amusedly contemptuous of her presence. A little poke might help clarify the situation.

She still hadn't dealt with the gnome enough to get a true feel for his limits, which meant she was still at a disadvantage even before taking into account that the little man was vastly older than her—or maybe even human civilization.

"Got your message." Shay reached into her pocket to produce the orb. "And thanks for the assist. It was damned helpful there, Rumpelstiltskin."

The gnome's expression didn't change. "I'm not Wrinkledforeskin."

"I said 'Rumpelstiltskin,' you dick."

"You humans are so strange," he remarked in an amused tone.

Shay sighed and shook her head, not sure if the gnome had actually misheard her.

"Look, the point is, I owe you, and I always pay my debts—especially when they are to my local gnome, who has hooked me up more than once. I know you don't give a shit about cash, but I already proved with the adamantine that I can get hard-to-find items."

A hungry smile appeared on his face. "Hard-to-find items?"

Shay squared her shoulders. "Yep. I'm not going to Oriceran, but if it's on Earth, I can get it."

"I have no need of items from you. Not yet."

Shay narrowed her eyes. "I'm not killing anyone for you."

The gnome snorted. "I'm the one who left you the note about misuse, remember? I have no need of an assassin."

"Then what do you want?"

Tubal-Cain's face softened, and he folded his hands behind his back. "The problem, you see, is that Earth is annoying."

"Well, I agree. I'm sure Oriceran's annoying, too. What's that have to do with anything?"

"You've demonstrated the ability to find not only things but also information, Miz Carson. I want to take advantage of that to have you find a missing cousin of mine."

"Not saying I won't help, but don't you have some sort of tracking spell you can use? That seems like that'd be easier than hiring a tomb raider to moonlight as a private detective."

The gnome shrugged. "Oh, I've access to myriad enchantments, spells, and artifacts with such functions." His face twisted in irritation. "But they have all proven less than useful. With your skills and penchant for running into dangerous situations and managing not to die, I thought you might be helpful in this regard."

"Is your cousin in trouble?" Shay inquired.

"Not necessarily, but he might be. Maybe not. You never know."

"Okay then, you need me to locate him?"

"Yes. He used to go by 'Bosvid,' but I can't be sure what name he might be using on Earth now." Tubal-Cain frowned. "I'll be honest with you. I'm a recent immigrant, and my connections aren't always as strong as I'd like."

Shay blinked, surprised the gnome would confide something like that to her. Trust, or perhaps desperation.

"Okay, this sounds doable. You have any information about your cousin that might be helpful besides his name? Are you sure he's even on Earth? I'm a badass tomb raider and researcher, but I've never been to Oriceran, and I don't even have a reliable means of getting there."

"That's not a problem," Tubal-Cain replied. "What little I have managed to find points to my cousin having been on Earth as recently as three hundred years ago."

As recently *as three hundred years ago? You've got to be fucking kidding me.*

Shay sighed. "Anything else?"

"Yes. I can narrow down the search area considerably."

"Oh? Where was he last seen?"

"Europe." Tubal-Cain gave a triumphant smile.

Shay resisted a groan, again unsure if the gnome was serious or screwing with her.

"I'll start poking around," she offered. "And see what I can turn up."

"Excellent. Is there anything else you want from me? I do appreciate the difficulty in finding Bosvid, and I think it's worth more than just a loan of an artifact."

"Well, if you're offering, a magical lockpick would come in handy." Shay shrugged.

"Very well. I may know of something you could use. Come back to me with the information, and I'll see what I can do."

Shay's eyes fluttered open and she rolled onto her side on the bed, bumping into the solid mass of muscle that was James Brownstone. She watched him for a moment, a soft smile playing on her lips.

When she'd stopped at his newly rebuilt house the night before, she hadn't been sure about pushing their relationship forward, but now that they'd slept together an unfamiliar sensation filled her: contentment.

It's been a long time since I've felt this calm.

Before she might have been able to pretend they were not in a relationship, but now they were lovers, and she'd even brought over her favorite crystal skull toothbrush holder. The whole situation was turning dangerously domestic.

Shay ran her fingers through the sleeping man's hair.

"Guess two fucked-up people like us were bound to end up together, huh, James?" Shay whispered.

A quiet chuckle followed and she smiled, savoring the use of his first name instead of his last.

Their relationship might last a few weeks, or until their deaths. Considering their lifestyles, there was also the distinct possibility that their deaths might only be a few weeks away.

Shay didn't care. For now, she'd be satisfied to hold onto the small slice of happiness she'd found with James Brownstone.

"Okay, I definitely did not expect that look," Shay announced as she approached the office.

Peyton sat at his desk, his orange tabby draped over his head like a hat. The researcher turned toward Shay and Osiris leapt to the ground with a loud yowl.

Shay stared down at the cat. "Seriously?"

The cat paused, one front paw in the air for a moment as he watched Shay as if waiting for her to make a move. After a few seconds, he darted through her legs and ran out of the office.

"Aww, he was just getting comfortable." Peyton sighed.

"Spoil your cat too much, and you'll regret it." Shay pointed at the computer. She cleared her throat and asked the question she really wanted to know. "Still no sign?"

Peyton looked up and shook his head. "Nope, no sign of Lily, no sign of trouble. She may just be gone. Gray ghost is in the wind."

"Maybe it's for the best." Shay did her best to shake off the feeling that something wasn't quite right. Did Lily see something in the near future that spooked her? "Got a little side job for you. Something perfect for your skills."

"Liking the sound of this. Or maybe I should be afraid of the sound of this? Give me the details, and I'll figure it out."

Shay shrugged. "It's not a big deal. Tubal-Cain wants

me to find some cousin of his, a gnome named Bosvid. He was last seen on Earth in Europe about three hundred years ago."

Peyton scoffed. "Oh, only three hundred years ago? Is that all?"

Shay shrugged. "I didn't say it'd be easy, just that you'd be perfect for it."

"Okay. And what am I getting paid for this little side job?"

Shay laughed, then blinked. "Wait, you're serious? You're not getting paid anything. With the percentage slice I've started giving you on jobs you're making more than enough to keep you in silly clothes and costumes for years, and that's before I consider how you've been fleecing James."

"It's just a modest cover charge for services rendered."

"Did you charge him when you helped him out with the AET?"

"Well, no. That was for you, though, not him."

Shay patted Peyton on the shoulder. "This is just some research for me. Not asking you to break into any government computers or try and translate weird alien writing. I remember how shortly after I first fake-killed you, you were bragging about your magical research skills. Now you're whining?"

"I do know a lot of people," Peyton grumbled, "but I'm not a miracle worker."

"Never too late in life to pick up new titles."

"Okay." Peyton sighed. "And that's all you have to work from, the name of a gnome who might have been in Europe three hundred years ago?"

"Sure." Shay walked toward the office door. "I'm gonna be out of town with James visiting Alison this weekend. If you turn up anything important, just text me. I don't need a play by play. I want to know about it once you've located him or his grave, but until then I don't give a shit."

Peyton saluted her. "Yes, ma'am."

7

Peyton's computer beeped with an alert—another hit for one of his bots. He smiled at the window that popped up on his second monitor.

He wasn't sure why he'd waited so long to set up another monitor. On some level he'd been convinced Shay would get rid of him, fatally or otherwise. With his apartment and cat, and even Shay's relationship, everything now felt more stable—or at least as stable as a life could be when a man was hiding in LA after faking his death in New York and working for a tomb raider who had faked her own death.

"That's what I like to see." Ten seconds passed as he scrolled through results. "Actually, I'd like to see half of that. Maybe a third. Need to refine these algos more."

His bots had returned a tsunami of search results to provide the raw material for further processing by various algorithms. Drowning in hits was still a problem, even with the programs and machine-learning tools he had at his disposal.

Finding a gnome in hiding who had been living on Earth for centuries was an interesting challenge that was leaning heavily on his non-technical skills. His searches, automated or otherwise, were focused far more on folklore and legends than simple record searches.

One problem was that human societies had defined magical beings a myriad of ways prior to the full return of magic. An elf from Oriceran might look very different than a gnome, but a small village in eighteenth-century Germany might have run into a gnome and called it an elf. It wasn't like he could just pop onto Google and type "Bosvid the gnome."

The rest of his plan was brilliant in its simplicity of idea, if not its execution. Step one: gather raw data with bots using customized algorithms. Step two: cross-reference the gathered data and filter using algorithms and manual inspection. Step three: verify Bosvid's location. Step four: bask in Shay's praise of his awesome research skills.

The raw data so far was promising, but a gnome who had hidden for centuries wasn't going to be listed in some cutesy newspaper article about local characters. Therefore, Peyton had unleashed an army of bots to hit all corners of the web, hidden or otherwise.

He's a gnome, not some DOD White Hat. It's not like he'd even think to take measures to hide his presence from computer searches until recently.

Peyton grinned, the thought buoying his confidence.

His fingers ran across the keyboard as he passed a batch of search results through his first set of filtering algorithms.

Shay'd been wrong when she'd described the job. When someone searched for a person on the internet who didn't want to be found, it often led to hacking into servers. Passive data collection wouldn't cut it.

People in the government had known about Oriceran before the general public had, which meant at least some of them might have access to hidden information concerning the wayward gnome.

Project Houdini had been mentioned in some of the Project Nephilim files. Peyton couldn't be sure, but the name made him think it had something to do with magic. He doubted the government was spending a lot of money refining escape artistry. A few probes into governmental systems wouldn't hurt.

Osiris stepped into the room and stretched before curling up in the corner near a floor vent.

Peyton smiled at the cat. "You got any ideas? Can you hunt out the gnome for me?"

The tabby meowed.

The researcher's phone chimed. "Oh, yeah, forgot about that. Don't want to get my priorities messed up." He picked up the phone.

His eyes widened. The message on the screen was far more important than the location of a gnome.

"I got a response, Osiris!" Peyton cheered.

His cat rested his head on his paws. He didn't even bother to look up at the man, as if signaling his utter apathy toward the human's excitement.

Peyton couldn't wipe the grin off his face as looked at his important message...from a dating app.

Hi. It says we're supposed to be a good match, and I liked your message. Sure, I think we could go out for drinks sometime.

After his last disastrous attempts at dating, Peyton had almost given up and convinced himself that dating wasn't a possibility. That he'd have to sacrifice it to stay alive. He'd even convinced himself that Shay had been right, and maybe he *should* be hiding in the warehouse.

But that was bullshit.

Shay had pissed off far more people than he had in *both* of her lives, and was living a full life. She traveled, operated in public, went out with friends, and was even dating a famous bounty hunter. If *she* could have a life, *he* could have a life.

Not that she needed to know about *his* life.

Another alert popped up from a different dating app. Much like searching for a missing gnome, finding the right woman required patience and a wide variety of tools.

Peyton dashed off a few quick messages. He didn't want to get himself too excited until he'd verified that the dating responses weren't from bots, but it was a good start.

He set the phone down and returned his attention to his computer. Several filtered results filled a small window on his second monitor.

Peyton nodded. "Okay, these are definitely looking promising. Huh, what's this? Guess it's time to take a poke around a few National Reconnaissance Office servers."

Peyton yawned and looked at the two side-by-side satellite photos before clicking over to the next comparison set.

A day of gathering and filtering data had already yielded a few possibilities. A few research strands had suggested that someone named Bosvid had come to the United States from Germany right after the end of the American Civil War, but the only proof of that was a few lines on some county tax records in Maine.

That would be easy to ignore, but a trail of unusual events and legends starting in Maine and heading west corresponded with the years following the arrival of Bosvid. Those were revealed not by Peyton's searching or the Project Houdini information, but by a file recovered from a hidden IRS server—a document entitled *The Difficult Issue of Magical Tax Evasion: A Historical Perspective*.

No matter how much the world changed, death and taxes remained constant.

Peyton chuckled at the thought as he continued looking at the satellite photos.

Several convergent lines of evidence from archaeologists, historians, and government sources pointed him toward Iowa, not all that far outside of Des Moines. He magnified a few sections of the satellite photos and clicked to inspect images taken on different dates.

Too perfect. The images hadn't changed. He'd managed to gather dozens of satellite images of what was allegedly a large farm, but all the images looked exactly the same, regardless of the date or the source satellite, including the layout and density of the rows of corn and the exact positions of the vehicles.

Even if the farmers parked the same place every night,

he'd expect at least one daytime picture of the vehicles out in the field. The presence of non-fallow fields argued against the idea the farm was abandoned.

Suspicious. Damned suspicious.

Peyton brought up another picture, an aerial photograph taken in the 1950s. The closer distance changed aspects of the image, but the layout of the buildings and corn remained the same.

He narrowed his eyes. Other than the angle, everything else was identical. He ran an image comparison analysis between the 1950s photo and the satellite images.

Chance of match: 96.5%.

Peyton isolated only the vehicles in the older photo and then compared them to the satellite images.

Chance of match: 99.7%.

He chuckled. A farmer might take good care of his equipment, but he doubted he was using the same trucks and tractors for eighty years.

"Iowa, though?" Peyton shook his head. "Why would the gnome be in Iowa?"

Shay probably wouldn't care if she found out I was dating, as long as I made it clear I was lying to the women. She's let me move out of the warehouse.

Maybe Brownstone knows someone? Then again, Brownstone is dating Shay, so I don't think I want him to try and hook me up with anyone. I couldn't handle a woman like Shay.

Peyton shuddered at the thought.

He nodded to himself as he pulled off the highway in

his rented Toyota SUV. He hit a country road leading to what was supposed to be Morris Farms. Their web presence was non-existent, something that made Peyton just twitch thinking about it. He only knew the name because of local property tax records.

Someone was hiding something at Morris Farms, and they'd gone through the trouble to use magic or technology to hide from satellites—which meant they knew what they were doing.

The road grew bumpier, and Peyton blew out a breath. Shay might understand about him dating someone and hanging out in LA, but running off to Iowa by himself would probably earn him another death threat or the return of the cubicle apartment.

"She doesn't need to know," he murmured. "It's not like she's going to demand I lead her through the search process point by point."

He nodded to himself, satisfied with the need for a little lie-by-omission. Shay kept plenty of things from him. She was even keeping secrets from her boyfriend. A few secrets and lies here and there helped the world spin smoother.

Fifteen minutes of driving brought Peyton farther down the bumpy country road and within five miles of Morris Farms according to his GPS. He hadn't seen a sign or another vehicle for the last ten minutes.

This is as good as time as any.

Peyton slowed his SUV and pulled to the side of the road. Driving straight into a farm that might be hidden by magic and asking around would probably end with him being turned into a toad.

He killed the engine and pressed a button to open the

back hatch. Whistling, Peyton wandered to the back to pull out one of the drones he'd brought. Whatever magic was being used to shield the farm obviously worked from thousands of feet up, but he suspected a closer inspection might reveal the truth.

"Just here for a few photos," Peyton murmured to himself. "In and out. No fuss, no muss, no guns, no getting turned into a toad. No guy calling me bad names in German."

A few minutes later the drone buzzed away from Peyton, flying low to the ground. He sat inside the car taking deep breaths, his attention focused on the feed on his phone.

What if the gnome has some sort of spell where he can zap me through the drone?

Peyton's stomach tightened and he swallowed, remembering how he'd almost ended up getting killed in a parking lot in Madison on a previous venture outside LA.

Surviving the experience had only reinforced in Peyton's mind that he harbored no hidden danger fetish. Shay could fight crazy Australian monsters in the desert, but he'd mostly stick to his computer.

Peyton slapped a hand to his forehead. "What the fuck am I doing? The Midwest is my kryptonite." He took several deep breaths and shook his head. "Nope. Keep it together. Sometimes you just have to verify things on site. I just won't get near them. There have been no mysterious deaths reported in the area, so it's not like the gnomes are killing everyone who snoops around them." He winced. "Unless they covered up the deaths with magic. Oh, shit. Maybe I *will* die a toad."

The drone continued zooming along fifty feet off the ground. Few trees lined the road, and the open, flat land offered nowhere to hide. After a couple of miles, Peyton stopped the drone's advance and increased its altitude.

Being closer to the farm would have been preferable, but the custom camera he'd installed would get him decent images even at a distance. He was there to verify the presence of the gnome, not sell pictures to tabloids.

Peyton magnified and enhanced the image of the farm. He saw nothing but the pure excitement of rows and rows of corn, along with ancient trucks and tractors.

Peyton focused on one of the trucks and then a tractor. The old designs were consistent with what he could make out in the satellite photos, but the vehicles looked spotless, as if they'd been sitting in a vault for decades and had been deployed to the farm the day before.

"Yeah, that's not suspicious at all."

The image shimmered for a moment.

"What the hell was that?" He repositioned the drone, but the shimmer didn't reappear.

Shay has to concentrate to find the gnome's shop in the mall, and she said the gate at Alison's school screws with people's minds. There are tons of other examples of mental and physical illusion magic that can be beaten by knowing what you are looking for. Could the gnome be pulling that off even through a drone feed?

Peyton gritted his teeth and stared at the image, ignoring the feel of the phone in his hand and the flight data. He let his eyes grow unfocused like he was trying to spot a hidden picture in a colorful pattern, but kept his mind on the idea of gnomes and Bosvid.

Something moved on the phone, breaking his concentration. He wasn't even sure what he'd seen since the feed revealed the same boring eternally-unchanged farm as before. That might be proof of something strange, but it wasn't proof of a hidden gnome.

Peyton rewound the drone footage. A distortion had hit the feed, but he had no idea of the source. He rewound the footage again and started advancing it frame by frame.

Corn, tractors, trucks...nothing special. There wasn't even a fake human or two in the images.

"What the hell?"

Peyton blinked at a single frozen frame. If he backed up or advanced one frame, there was nothing but the same unchanging farm. The image in between was a slice of a different reality.

Dozens of gnomes wandered the farm, many sitting around long tables that didn't appear in any of the other images. Although some of the rows of corn remained, many newer buildings with odd curving designs stood in what should have been corn fields. There were no tractors or trucks.

"Huh," Peyton murmured. "So I didn't just find Bosvid, I found an entire hidden gnome colony." He grinned. "I'm so damned good."

8

Shay nibbled on her salad, smirking at James. He was glaring at his salad as if the very concept of a non-meat-based course offended him. The man needed to get over it. The nice little family diner they'd picked for their meal had something for everyone, and she wasn't going to eat barbeque or burgers every meal. She didn't even want pizza for every meal, and she adored pizza.

You're going to win in the long run anyway, James, since Alison's trying to eat more meat. Soon, we'll never go to a place that isn't a steakhouse or barbeque joint. I'm with you, James, but I'm never going to love barbeque like you. She felt a pang, remembering Lily and shook it off. She had only known the girl for a short amount of time. Let it go. Everyone ends up where they belong in the end, anyway.

Alison sipped her lemonade. "I'm so happy you could both come. I wasn't sure with all the...stuff you both have going on." She laughed. "Crazy stuff."

Stuff. Yeah, that's how I'd describe killing a cartel and researching James' alien shit.

Shay glanced between the girl and the bounty hunter. They hadn't told Alison about his alien background, but given her soul-sight, she might already have some idea. That secret wasn't Shay's to share, though. James would tell Alison when the time was right.

He shrugged. "Sorry I've been busy, kid. Things have been cleaned up for now, though. Gonna relax for a few days. Maybe even a few weeks."

"Me, too," Shay offered. "Not the relaxing for a few weeks thing, just sorry I've been busy."

Alison smiled. "The important thing is that you're both here now, and no bad guys are coming after Dad."

James snorted. "There will always be bad guys coming for me. That's just my life."

Shay elbowed him and shot him a glare. "Don't be a dick."

He shrugged. "But no bad guys right now, and not the Harriken. Don't even know if there are any left."

Alison set her fork down. "I'm not naïve. I get that you're never going to be as safe as some guy working in the office. I know that you can't give up your work, but just be careful, Dad. That's all I'm asking."

"I'm *always* careful. If it's a serious bounty, I take proper precautions. It's not like I'm gonna drive to some city for barbeque and then go after some high-level bounty half-assed prepared. You don't have to worry about me, kid."

Shay snickered.

"Well, good." Alison nodded as if satisfied with the answer, or maybe the soul energy she saw. The girl looked at Shay and James for a moment, a bright smile on her face. "Anything else you want to tell me about?"

Shit, does she know we're together? I guess it's not a secret or anything, but I don't really want to talk about it, either. It's just kind of weird. If we say anything, she'll be able to tell we're lying. A teen who can see lies—perfect. Why couldn't I have had that power when I was her age?

James grunted. "Oh, yeah, forgot to tell you."

Alison's smile grew. "Oh?"

Seriously, James? You're just gonna come out and say it?

"Yeah," James continued. "The lawyer I've got working on the adoption says sh…things are finally moving along again. According to him, the process will be completed by the end of the summer. He can't see anything else that would hold it up."

"I'm so glad to hear that. I already call myself 'Alison Brownstone,' but I want it to be official, so everyone in the country and the world knows."

Shay lifted her coffee mug to her face to hide her relief at the direction of the conversation. Discussing adoption was safe, and wouldn't lead to any awkward conversations about where Shay was sleeping some nights.

James frowned. "Sorry it's taking so long. It's my fault for not being normal."

Well, that and the fact that we killed her father. Shay resisted saying that aloud. Whatever changes to her perspective on life in recent months, she didn't regret helping to kill Alison's biological father. The bastard had sold his own wife to be tortured by gangsters and had only been stopped from doing the same to his daughter by

James. The only regret Shay had was that he hadn't suffered more.

Alison giggled. "It's a big legal thing, Dad. It's not really taking that long, and the important thing is that it'll happen eventually." She turned toward Shay with a smile on her face, but her eyes as unfocused as always. "Someday I hope you can be my mom and not just my aunt. Shay Brownstone is a cool name, too."

James grunted. Shay twitched. Alison *knew*. She had to know.

Had James told her? Then again, would he even think to? Maybe she just saw it. Did people in relationships have some sort of weird soul energy signatures?

Shay shrugged and forced a smile. "You never know what the future's gonna bring, Alison. But enough about us! Why don't you catch us up on what's going on at school?"

"Sure! Izzie said something hilarious the other day…"

Shay settled in to listen, something at the edge of her mind poking her and not allowing her to embrace the comfort of the situation.

Something else is going on here. This family shit shouldn't freak me out so much, especially since the idea sounds so nice.

Shay bit down a laugh. Living a life focused on her instincts had made her recent forays into introspection uncomfortable, but that discomfort didn't change some of the truths she'd uncovered.

I'm freaked out at the idea of being happy and having friends and family who care for me. Who knew?

Shay lifted her fork and eyed the moist-looking chocolate cake. Her chicken-fried steak had left little room in her stomach, but she still wanted a bite or two. Not that she was worried. Given how much she worked out, she could down chocolate cake at every meal and not gain an ounce.

Her phone vibrated, and she set down the fork. A frown creased her features. The call was from Peyton.

I just want some cake, but then again, he wouldn't call me on a visit to Alison for random bullshit.

Is this about the gnome? I told him I didn't need to know all the details, and I doubt he found that gnome already. It might take us months to locate that little prick.

"Problem?" James inquired.

Shay shook her head. "I don't think so, or at least nothing important. I just have to take a call. I'll be right back."

James nodded, and Alison smiled.

The tomb raider didn't answer until she was out of the restaurant and around the corner. She leaned against the rough brick of the wall and brought the phone to her ear.

"This better be important," Shay barked into the phone. "I'm trying to do fam… I can't always visit Alison, you know, so when I'm off the clock, I want to be *off the clock*."

Her lingering worries over an uncomfortable future of happiness and familial bliss sank underneath the immediate darker and harder currents. A bright future might lie ahead, but taking down the Nuevo Gulf Cartel didn't mean that future was secure.

"I'm sorry," Peyton replied. "I wouldn't have called if it wasn't important."

"Does it involve someone dying? Someone I give two shits about?"

"Yeah. Well, maybe. You see, I've got a lot of alerts set up for a lot of things. Not just job stuff, but anything that looks like someone is sniffing around you or your alias too closely. I also have a bunch set up for my family."

"Yeah, I know that, and I remember you freaking out about your brother. So what, your brother is snooping around again? I thought we discussed this? Those guys aren't at your level. They're not a problem."

Shay kept her voice steady and casual. She couldn't have Peyton panicking when she was thousands of miles away. He might end up doing something stupid like flying to the East Coast to try and handle his brother alone, and no matter how slick Peyton believed he was, he wouldn't last long in the field against someone who knew he was coming. Her specialty was kicking ass. His was support.

Shit. I'm probably going to have to kill his brother in the end. Have to be careful, though. If he ends up conveniently dead when people know he was poking around it might bring even more attention, and we just got the government off my ass."

"No," Peyton answered, "not Randy. Way worse. Someone we *should* worry about. Someone even *you* should be worried about."

Shay snorted. "Talk about dramatic. Who's the big threat?"

"Francois Durand."

"What about him? You said he likes to keep a low profile. I don't even know the next time we might end up on a job related to an artifact he'd care about. Not saying I don't care at all, just saying that he's pretty low on my priority list right now."

Peyton sighed. "Wish I could say the same about him."

"Huh?"

"My alerts. They weren't flagging Durand's activities. They went off because someone is digging into you in a big way online, or to be clear, digging into Aletheia. When I poked into it, I found it was Durand. The guy's suddenly obsessed with your tomb-raiding career. He's going all out, including fake accounts to try to gather information."

Shay scoffed. "That doesn't mean much. My reputation has skyrocketed in a short time. Of course, I'm gonna get a few people looking into me and wanting to know my deal."

"Yeah, but why now? I don't buy that he wouldn't check at all after everything you've done and suddenly decided this weekend that you're worth his interest. Something changed."

Shay blew out a breath as she thought about the possibilities. "Yeah, something *did* change."

"What?"

"You started looking into him," Shay clarified. "The guy is so low-profile that you said he was a ghost. He's probably got a few alarms of his own set up."

Peyton groaned. "No, no, no. Seriously?"

"Just saying."

"No," Peyton insisted. "That can't be it. I get that he might be spooked about someone checking into him, but what I did wouldn't be linked to Aletheia. Unless this guy is the literal God of Computers, there's no way he'd think to look your way."

"Then he's got another reason," Shay mused. "Something we don't know about yet."

"He's working with Project Nephilim, which means he's got to be interested in your stone. Of course, he's going to want to collect more of them."

"Maybe, but it's not like anyone knows I have the stone—not even the Professor or his Elf Mafia buddy."

"Sure," Peyton offered. "But they know you've recovered at least one on their behalf, and from the way you talked with them, they might have figured out you have another."

Shay frowned. "Even if they were behind Durand in some weird-ass roundabout way, it'd make no sense to play those kinds of games. The Professor has his secrets, but I think that if he really wanted the stone, he'd just come to me and offer a buttload of cash or an artifact exchange."

"What about the other guy? Correk?"

"Who the fuck knows? I've started checking a little more into his background and his name keeps popping up in odd places, but nothing concrete so far. Plus, I don't see why a light elf would hire some human contractor to do his dirty work for him."

"They hired *you*, didn't they?"

Shay laughed. "First, I'm badass. Second, the Professor did the hiring. The elf was just along for the ride."

"Okay, that still brings us back to the original question." Peyton sighed. "What do we do?"

"Do what you do best." Shay chuckled. "Redirect that shit. Just because Durand's looking around doesn't mean he needs to find me, and this can end up being a *good* thing."

"How is having this guy looking for you, even through your alias, a good thing?"

"Because now we know he's interested in me. Fore-warned is forearmed." Shay pushed away from the wall. "And now we can take precautions."

"That makes sense."

"Do you need me to come back?" She didn't want to, but if her assistant was that freaked out, she might be forced to return to LA.

There was silence for a few beats before Peyton answered, "No. I'm good." The confidence had crept back into his voice. "It's like you said before with my brother. If Durand were as good at computer stuff as I am, I wouldn't have even seen him coming. I can send him on a wild goose chase to Abu Dhabi, and by the time he figures it out you'll have found every single alien artifact on this planet."

Shay laughed. "Sounds good. See you in a couple of days."

"See you."

Shay ended the call and smirked to herself.

I disabled your Deadman's Switch, Peyton, and you haven't figured it out. I'm a cut above Durand and the losers your brother hired.

She slipped her phone back into her purse and went back into the diner. French retrieval specialists, alien arti-facts, and even vicious Russian witches could wait. Her man and this teenage girl needed her.

9

S hay stared down at the disassembled pistol on the table in front of her. Field stripping a weapon wasn't exactly a fun and sexy time, but properly cleaning a weapon cut down on reliability issues.

Back when she was a killer she had mostly confined her jobs to cities and towns. Since becoming a tomb raider, she'd ended up on every continent including Antarctica, in every type of environment. Spending so many days in the Outback had also reminded her that she wouldn't always be able to grab new gear.

Having a gun jam in the middle of a fight because she had been slacking wasn't a risk she was willing to take.

The wall leading to the Annex groaned open, and Peyton emerged a moment later with a few different coats draped over his arm.

Anything that was on the general racks wasn't critical to the prepared identity packages, so it wouldn't hurt her to let the man play dress-up on occasion as long as he cleaned up after himself.

Peyton stopped and blinked, obviously surprised by her being there. "Uh, hi, Shay."

She chuckled. "Did I forget to tell you I was coming?"

"The last message you sent said you'd talk to me in Warehouse Two tomorrow. I wasn't sure if you were even flying back tonight." He tapped a code on the keypad and the wall slid shut. "Everything okay in Virginia?"

"Peachy."

"And you just decided to stop by Warehouse Three and clean guns?"

"Yeah, actually."

Peyton tilted his head to the side. "I miss her too. I was getting used to all the flipping and twirling and swinging through the warehouse."

"I'm over it," muttered Shay, lifting the gun.

Peyton took a deep breath. "If this is some sort of veiled threat, I'm not getting it."

Shay rolled her eyes. "The universe doesn't revolve around you." She patted the table. "You should learn how to do this eventually, but I don't have the patience to teach you right now. Or probably ever. That's what the internet's for."

Peyton moved to a nearby table to lay down the coats, discomfort lingering on his face. "Since you're here, I suppose I should let you know I found the gnome."

"Oh, that's cool. I—" Shay looked up from the pistol receiver she was cleaning. "Are you *shitting* me?"

"Nope. I know exactly where is. He's in a gnome colony

in Iowa. It's hidden by magic that cloaks it from most satellites and other photos, but it's definitely there."

Shay set the cloth and receiver on the table. "*Iowa?* Why Iowa?"

"Why not? It's not like it makes more sense for a gnome to be in England or something."

The tomb raider shrugged. "Good point."

"Maybe they really like corn? Do they even *have* corn on Oriceran?"

Shay thought that over for a few seconds. "I honestly have no fucking clue." She smiled. "Hell, I'm impressed, Peyton! I thought that shit was gonna take months, but you pulled it off in your spare time when I wasn't around."

He stood up straighter. "I think you forget how badass I am at times."

"You're skilled, but you're not badass. Badass would mean you could find Lily." She saw him wince and wanted to take it back... mostly. "And not to be a dick, but you confirmed our particular gnome was there, right, and not just a bunch of corn-gobbling gnomes?"

Peyton's confidence fled. "I traced him there by records, but I don't know how I could confirm his presence. Do you even know what he looks like?"

"Nope. I wasn't given a description, just the name."

"Yeah, so there's a lot of gnomes there, and all the other lines of evidence point there. Sounds good enough to me." Peyton shrugged. "It wasn't like I got close enough to ask them, just close enough that my drone's flight time wasn't too long."

"Oh, fuck. You didn't..." Shay narrowed her eyes. "Close enough to ask them?"

Peyton nodded. "Yeah, I was…" He winced. "Oh shit." He face-palmed.

Shay glared at him. "Let me get this straight. Not only did you leave LA, but you went all the way to Iowa to poke your nose into a nest of very magical beings?"

"Uh, yes? Look, I was careful, and I needed to go there to confirm things anyway. The evidence was decent but getting a few drone images actually proves there are gnomes there. Otherwise, all we would have is a suspiciously unchanging farm, and your gnome might have blown that off." Peyton slapped a hand over his chest. "I had to go, for the good of the job."

Shay looked down at the table and shook her head. She'd never felt such an odd combination of pride and rage in her life.

"I'm not gonna say you didn't do a good job, because you obviously did. You found a gnome colony, and yeah, our guy's probably there. Shit, you even got pictures, and I can show those to Tubal-Cain." She lifted her head and tried her best to resist the urge to march over to Peyton and lay him out with a punch for taking the risk. "But you can't just—"

A loud klaxon sounded from Peyton's phone.

"What the fuck was that?" Shay inquired mildly.

Peyton slid his phone out of his pocket. "My search alarm."

"Oh. Is it that French asshole again?"

"One sec." Peyton swiped and tapped with a teenager's frenzy. "No, it's not Durand."

"Who is it then?"

"Not a hundred percent sure, but they aren't looking for you. They're looking for *me*. I'm going to have to lay more false trails. It must be my brother's guys." Peyton rubbed his temples. "Damn it. I must have fucked up, and someone saw me in Iowa. Shit."

Shay shook her head. "I'm not all that happy about you wandering off to Iowa by yourself, but it's a coincidence."

"A coincidence?"

"Yeah. Come on, it's not like your brother has a bunch of guys hanging out in Iowa waiting for you."

Peyton frowned as he tapped through a few more messages. "I should grab my laptop from my car and start handling this crap."

"Yeah, you should." Shay shook her head. "But this only makes it clear that you need to decide, Peyton."

"Decide what?"

Shay locked gazes with him. "You understand what's gonna happen if your brother finds you?"

Peyton swallowed. "He'll kill me."

Shay shook her head. "Nah, always remember he's too much of a pussy for that. He's not gonna kill you. I'd have an ounce of respect for him if he had the balls to do that." She sucked in a breath. "Instead, he's gonna have you killed. What you need to decide is if you still want your family or if you're done with them."

"What are you saying, exactly?"

"I'm saying we can't even begin to end this shit if you haven't made up your mind about who your actual enemies are."

Peyton heaved a sigh. "Screw the laptop. I'm going back

to Warehouse Two to set up on my main computer and take care of these assholes." He shuffled toward the door.

"Think about what I said," Shay called. She picked up the receiver she'd been cleaning before. "In the end, this kind of shit always comes down to you or them."

Her phone rang, and she sighed.

"What now?"

Shay pushed into the Leanan Sídhe, a frown on her face. It'd been a while since she'd last been in the pub, and her shoulders and neck tightened at the dense crowd. She wouldn't have been surprised if some asshole strolled in someday and took a shot at the Professor and escaped because of all the drunks choking the place.

Smite-Williams always appeared at ease in the place, even trusting the owner enough to store some of his delivered artifacts for short periods. Magical defenses must have been set up that Shay couldn't perceive.

Or maybe the old drunk just really liked the beer here.

The tomb raider maneuvered through the crowd, sparing an occasional glance toward the door. That was the other annoying part of meeting the Professor in the pub. She could almost never practice defensive seating since the man always sat in such a way where *he* could see the door, but her back was to it.

I swear, Professor, if I end up getting shot in the back, I'll come back and fucking haunt you until you have to hire a witch to drive off my ghost.

The silver-haired man sat ruddy-faced in his usual

booth, a happy smile plastered on his face. Father O'Banion didn't usually come out during business, but it wouldn't surprise Shay if he did.

She slipped into a seat across from the Professor and shrugged. "You said it was urgent, so I came."

"Aye, Miz Carson. It's urgent. Would you be available to leave for a job tomorrow morning? It's in Paris."

Shay leaned forward with a coy smile on her face. Sometimes the Professor shouldn't have all the power.

"What if I said no?"

The Professor chuckled and took a sip of his beer. "Then you'd be throwing away millions of dollars and squandering some of my goodwill for no good reason." He set his glass down and shrugged. "Everything is, of course, your choice, as always."

"Not saying no, just curious about what would happen if I did."

"I see. Do you want to hear about the job?"

Shay shrugged. "Hard to turn it down or agree to it if I don't know what it is."

"Aye, that it would be. Are you familiar with the Order of the Silver Griffins?"

"A little. They were supposed to patrol a lot of this magic shit back before all hell broke loose."

The Professor gave a curt nod. "That's a succinct way of describing things. Yes, before every random fool could wander the streets with a wand, the Order aggressively controlled unauthorized magic, including keeping many powerful artifacts stored away. They used to have a vault for magical artifacts in Chicago under the Water Tower."

"Didn't that place burn down twenty years ago?"

"It was destroyed, yes, but it was hardly an accident. Further details aren't all that important right now, other than to note that among the artifacts that returned to circulation following the destruction of the Order's vault was the Scepter of Dagobert."

A waitress approached but turned away at the Professor's nod.

"Scepter of Dagobert?" Shay echoed. "That used to be part of the French regalia, but it disappeared during the Revolution, right?"

The Professor nodded and gulped down some more of his favorite amber liquid. "Aye, but it's not just a pretty stick, that's for certain. It's one of the oldest-known and most powerful wands."

"But you mentioned Paris. It's popped back up there?"

"Information has surfaced about a series of unusual occurrences on the streets of Paris, along with at least one sighting of something that resembled the Scepter. I believe that a very, very foolish witch or wizard has gotten their hands on it and are testing it out." He chuckled. "Unfortunately for them and us, it's too powerful. They're likely already channeling more magical energy than can be safely handled, and the consequences and side effects might prove very severe."

Shay frowned. "What kind of side effects?"

"The death of the wielder, for one."

"Big deal. We wait until they finish getting off on the big wand and collect it from their corpse." Shay shrugged.

"There's a chance they might take Paris with them, either through direct use of the wand or a flare of magic from it."

"Oh, yeah, that'd suck. I see your point."

Shay might regret what she was about to say, but she also couldn't deny its logic.

"What about bringing James in on this?"

The Professor's brow lifted. "Calling him James now? I see." A huge grin appeared.

Shay rolled her eyes. "Whatever. The point is, you're making it sound like some idiot kid is walking around with the magical equivalent of a nuke, and you've talked about them wandering the streets of Paris. This isn't a tomb raid, it's a hunt, and he's useful for that kind of shit on occasion."

The Professor chuckled. "Aye, the lad is, but he also has all the subtly of a volcano."

"Not disagreeing there, but what are you getting at?"

"I want the Scepter recovered, but I don't want to hear on the news about a massive magical battle in Paris. Various people interested in this matter are already having a hard time keeping too much information from leaking to the media."

Shay snorted. "Big deal. It's not like the old days. Everyone knows about magic. Why are they bothering to cover it up?"

"Aye, everyone *does* know about magic, which is why the interested parties have been able to spin the individual incidents as pranks or misunderstandings. But if people realize there's something more powerful going on, it could cause chaos. Then people will get hurt."

"Okay, I get it."

"Not only that, James isn't that good at keeping a low profile. He's famous now. If he shows up people will notice and focus on him and the info will come out, or the wielder of the Scepter of Dagobert might feel cornered and launch a massive surprise attack. Not only that, James would probably tell someone what he was doing if they politely inquired. You, on the other hand, are good at keeping a low profile and lying."

"You sure know how to sweet-talk a girl, Professor."

"In this matter, Miz Carson, I can assure you that those are very positive traits. Your…background prepares you for this job in a manner that James' doesn't."

Shay narrowed her eyes. She had always suspected the Professor knew about her first career and true past, but nothing would be gained by confronting him about it right now.

"I get it," Shay replied softly. "I go to Paris. I find the witch or wizard. Take them out, and recover the wand, all while keeping it quiet. Sound about right?"

"You don't have to kill them," the Professor clarified. "But I'm dubious that they'll give up such a powerful artifact willingly, so we must all do what we need to do to protect innocent people."

"Okay, and I'm assuming I need to go sooner rather than later. Earlier you mentioned leaving in the morning?"

"Aye. Time is of the essence, Miz Carson. You're willing to take on the job, then?"

Shay grinned. "Don't worry, Professor—you had me at 'millions of dollars.'"

He polished off the last of his beer. "You'll take commercial supersonic transport to Paris, but I've arranged for a private plane flying from a private airstrip for your return trip. It won't be supersonic, but this artifact is simply too powerful to risk flying around without special precautions. The arrangements I made have you flying out tomorrow morning at nine. That'll put you in Paris by sunset."

Shay pushed up from the table with a nod. "Then I'd better gather my shit. I've got a wand to find."

10

___

Shay would have preferred something a little more fashionable for her trip to Paris, but holsters and knife sheaths didn't pair well with dresses and heels. She was grateful for the unseasonably cool weather and falling night, which gave her an excuse to wear a stylish leather jacket to conceal her gear.

It was a nice jacket with killer shoulders, but it just wasn't a nice sexy dress. Fighting in the latter might prove difficult, though.

The need for stealth also necessitated a boring choice of a blue sedan, rather than a sexy convertible like the one she'd driven during her trip to Paris to recover the Golden Owl.

If someone did take note of her, they wouldn't see dark-haired Shay Carson, but auburn-haired photojournalist Kacy Lamont. She'd never had an opportunity to use the identity in her old killing days, even though she'd used other journalist identities.

She always found them useful. Journalists had an excuse to be wandering in strange places and asking pointed questions. Standing out didn't make them inherently suspicious.

Shay snorted. What was she thinking? She was having fun just because of some documents, a camera, a wig, and some contacts? The job might pay well, but it was still annoying as fuck.

Hunting down a witch in the middle of a major city isn't really my thing. If this wand is as dangerous as the Professor says, maybe I should have risked bringing James, after all.

The tomb raider sighed.

No, the Professor was right. He would have ended up doing some chest-thumping shit where he issued a public challenge, and we'd end up in some sort of battle royal with crazy local witches and wizards who wanted the wand, French cops, and who-knows-who-else, burning half of Paris down.

She loved the man, but James was a sledgehammer—and the situation called for a stiletto. Staying under the radar also meant that bringing the *tachi* was a no-go. She was driving for now, but she'd have to go after the wand wielder on foot once she found them and wandering the streets of Paris with a Japanese sword would attract a few eyeballs.

"Can you still hear me, Peyton?" Shay murmured into her throat mic as she entered a roundabout.

"Yeah, I can hear you. And your position from the GPS transponder is clear."

The mic was linked to a dedicated transmitter that interfaced with a VOIP comm line, and the earpiece was all but invisible. She could wander Paris talking to herself, and almost no one would notice unless they were right next to her.

"I like this," Peyton continued.

"Like what?"

"Riding shotgun on the mission."

"You're not riding shotgun. You're thousands of miles away."

"But I'm feeling it, you know? Controlling a drone, helping you navigate."

Shay rolled her eyes. "If I already knew where the mark was I wouldn't be doing this."

"Let me have my fun. Maybe someday I'll be hitting the streets with you."

"Not fucking likely."

Peyton muttered something under his breath.

"According to the follow-up info the Professor sent me," Shay began, "our boy or girl is mostly active at night."

"Makes sense, if they are trying things out and worried about someone coming after them."

Shay snickered. "Someone like me?"

"Well, yeah. Though they must be getting pretty cocky to draw that much attention."

"If someone handed you the ultimate magical tool, you'd be insufferable."

"At least I'd look good."

"That's a matter of opinion."

"You know you love my outfits."

Shay snorted. "Only because they keep you from being naked."

She exited the roundabout and did a quick one-handed pat-down, as if her gear might spontaneously teleport while she was driving. Pistol and mags, check. Adamantine knives, check. Low-power frequency jammer, check.

A magical lockpick would have been useful just in case, but the Professor's insistence that she leave all but immediately had prevented her from checking in with Tubal-Cain and informing him about the gnome colony in Iowa.

I'll worry about that after I've grabbed the wand. I bet it'll blow his little gnome mind that we found his cousin so quickly.

Shay turned onto a narrow tree-lined street. It'd be so easy to take out a car with an RPG or fireball on a street like that. Every time she came to Paris, she marveled at all the wonderful ambush locations the city presented. She'd taken advantage of several in her old career.

Guess it's a good thing they don't know I'm coming, so I'll be the only one getting the drop on people.

Shay slowed the car, taking in the view of a tall church in the distance. "The Professor's incident list is from all over Paris, both tourist and non-tourist places. Our wand-wielder sure gets around."

Peyton's keyboard-pounding was perfectly audible over the comm. "One second," he muttered. "Just let me re-check this list and the times of the events. Maybe I can see something you didn't."

"Not like I've got anywhere else to be."

Shay pulled into a small parking lot outside a café and idled while she waited. A few teenagers sauntered by but didn't even bother to glance her way.

It's the car. It's too damned boring. Sorry, guys.

"No pattern," Peyton offered after a few minutes. "But some of this stuff was close together and some across town. I mean, like our wizard or witch was across town minutes after doing something."

Shay drummed her fingers on the steering wheel. "Which means she's got mobility. Flight, maybe teleportation. Fuck, super-speed walking. None of the shit the Professor told me about indicates any of that. You'd think people would notice a flying person or someone zooming through the city."

"She might be able to turn invisible."

The tomb raider groaned. "That would be annoying." She glanced in the back at a box of equipment. "Don't know if infrared on the AR goggles will spot all types of invisibility, but it's at least worth a shot if it comes down to it."

Peyton laughed. "I'm so damned good."

"I think you're getting a little too excited about your invisibility theory."

"No, no. Nothing to do with that. I'm monitoring all sorts of sources for strange events. Just got a hit."

Shay pulled out of the parking lot and back onto the street. "Where and what?"

"Some chatter on social media about a ghost sighting in District One." Peyton rattled off the address.

Shay's heart raced, and she grinned.

Just like old times. Maybe I shouldn't like hunting someone down so much.

"On my way."

***

Shay pulled up to the address. A crowd of curious people

with their phones out surrounded a floating apparition of a young girl in a raggedy dress.

The girl floated back and forth, mouthing words silently.

"Wonder if this is an actual ghost or just an illusion?" Shay mused.

"Got another hit. Police reported a woman claiming that…" He laughed.

"What?" Shay snapped.

"She claims an anvil appeared out of nowhere and fell on her car."

"An anvil? As in a blacksmith's anvil?"

"Yep. In District 20." Peyton rattled off the address.

"Fuck, that's across town."

Peyton laughed. "You better get going, then."

Shay stood in front of her car and stared at the huge iron anvil now embedded in the hood of the very angry woman's car. The woman gesticulated wildly in front of a tired and confused-looking police officer. He looked like he wanted to retreat home and down a bottle of wine.

The tomb raider shook her head and slipped back into the driver's seat of her rental.

An hour later had brought with it several more incidents. No injuries, but definite damage, including a suspicious lightning strike.

"This shit is so random," Shay commented.

"Maybe they are just trying to see what they can do?" Peyton suggested.

"That's assuming they are actually planning any of this, and it isn't all weird side effects." Shay shook her head. "But we need to get ahead of this somehow. I can't just drive around the city all night."

"One sec. Let me check something."

Shay started the car back up and pulled into the street.

"I've got an idea," Peyton announced after a couple minutes.

"About?"

"I was looking at the earlier incidents, and I think I've figured out a pattern. It's not that your target is bouncing around randomly. It's not always even far away, relatively speaking. I think what they're doing is bouncing between high and low district numbers."

Shay blinked. "Okay. So our wand wielder is familiar with the layout of Paris, so probably a local. If that pattern is true, what's the next district."

"It should be something in District 8. I've got my drone on the way."

"And so am I."

"Got another hit," Peyton shouted.

"Tone it down, you're right in my ear."

"Sorry. The Fountain du Cirque in Jardin des Champs-Élysées is filling with blood, according to a panicky old lady. My drone is a few minutes out."

Shay grinned. "I know exactly where that is, and I'm damned close." She pressed the pedal to the floor.

I've got you now, asshole.

11

"I've tagged our target with the drone," Peyton announced. "Unless somebody else is carrying around a golden rod topped with a bird. Looks like a woman in a dress, from what I can tell at this distance. Also, uh, she shouldn't be hard to spot since she's glowing."

"Glowing?"

"Yeah. Glowing blue."

"You'd think people would have reported that shit."

Peyton laughed. "There aren't a huge number of people on the street, but I swear, most people she's running past are barely paying any attention. These Parisians have taken jaded to a whole new level. I think even in New York people would pay attention to a glowing woman with a golden rod."

"Well, not in Times Square."

"Yeah, not there."

Shay chuckled. "Anyway, where is she? We're on a

mission here, not filming a travel show. I need to know her location."

"Sure thing, Boss Lady."

"Don't call me that."

"Roger. She's southeast on Avenue Gabriel. She's almost to the intersection with Rue Boissy d'Anglas."

"Flying? Zooming? Jumping really high? What?"

"Nothing. She's just walking kind of fast, but not super fast. You know, like normal speed-walking. Maybe that's why no one cares."

Shay snorted. "*I* care."

She yanked on the wheel and made a hard right, cutting off another car. Their harsh horn cut through the night, but she ignored the other driver and barreled down the street, occasionally weaving between other vehicles. If she ended up getting a ticket later, her fake identity could deal with it. From what the Professor had told her about the Scepter, traffic shenanigans in defense of a major city would be worth it. Those, and the millions of dollars the Professor was offering.

Her car zoomed around a fountain, and Shay took another hard turn before screeching into a parking spot along the street. She whipped her head to the side just in time to catch a glimpse of a form outlined in blue light turning the corner.

You got sloppy, and I've got you.

The tomb raider bolted out of the car and sprinted after her target. She turned the corner. A young woman in a loose summer dress and ankle boots stood on the other side. A cerulean glow surrounded her, thin arcs of twisting energy extending from the glow's source: a golden rod topped with a hand holding the Earth and a bird. The Scepter of Dagobert.

"I've got eyes on the witch," Shay reported.

"I've got you both on the drone feed from three hundred feet up. No reinforcements coming her way from what I can see, and not a lot of people around."

"Good. Maybe I can stop this from getting too messy."

The witch spun toward Shay, sweat coating her arms and face. Her eyes glowed a solid azure, and her mouth twitched.

"It's not working," the witch spat in French. "I don't understand."

"What's not working?" Shay answered in English, hoping to draw the woman into switching languages.

The witch waved the Scepter, her eyes frantic. "The portals won't open for me now. I don't know why." Her English was French-accented but otherwise perfect.

"You're glowing," Shay pointed out. "Not a good sign. I'm not an expert, but maybe you're using too much power or some shit like that."

"Too much power?" She narrowed her eyes. "You don't seem surprised by this. Who are you? Is this your fault? Did *they* send you to stop me?"

"I'm about as magical as your typical rock in the park." Shay shrugged. "But, yeah, I've been looking for you—not that you've made yourself that hard to find with all the bullshit you've been doing."

"I needed to practice." The witch stepped back, taking Shay in with a sneer. "But you've come to take the Scepter from me, haven't you? You're lying, aren't you? You've done something, maybe poisoned the magic. Because you're jealous."

"I don't want it, but I know some people are concerned about it." The tomb raider's hand inched toward her holster. "Look, I've got nothing against you, chick, but I'd prefer you just hand it over. It's too fucking dangerous for you to run around with. Too fucking dangerous for *anyone*, from what *I* hear. Let me take it and hand it off so they can bury it at the bottom of some enchanted lake or pit or under a dragon's butt."

"Give up the Scepter of Dagobert?" The witch let out a cutting laugh. "Do you know how long I've been mocked? They told me I would never have great power?" She lifted the Scepter. "But I have it now. I found it—something they said was already gone—and I…I…" She shook her head and grimaced. "I *will* control it. I just need more time. No one will stop me. No one."

Killing the woman was the obvious solution, but Shay balked at the idea of gunning down someone who didn't seem to be a complete garbage fire of a human being. James' influence, perhaps.

Yeah, not the time to get soft.

Shay shook her head. "Just hand it over, and we can all walk away from this without anyone getting hu—"

A blue energy orb shot from the tip of the wand and Shay threw herself to the side. The orb passed over her and slammed into a nearby brick wall, the energy spreading out in several crawling strands.

Sonofabitch! Okay, so much for the nice-girl approach.

Shay whipped out her 9mm and opened fire, but the

bullets disappeared in a puff of blue mist as they struck the witch's body.

The witch didn't stand and fight. Instead, she rushed across the street.

"*Now* I wish I would have brought the damned sword. If these French people can ignore a glowing crazy woman, they could have ignored that."

The tomb raider sprinted after her, narrowly missing being hit by a car zooming down the road. Another car slammed on its brakes to avoid the fleeing witch.

Shay vaulted, rolled over the vehicle, and continued after the witch even as the driver shouted obscenities at her. A quick middle finger was her only response.

Her quarry ducked into a side street.

"Shit. I can't see her. Tell me you still have eyes on her, Peyton."

"Yep. She ran down the street about thirty feet in front of you and then broke left."

"Got it."

The sound of Shay's boots striking the asphalt echoed through the narrow alley. She emerged from the alley, her gun still out.

Years of instinct saved the tomb raider when she spotted a bright flash out of the corner of her eye. Throwing herself to the ground, she avoided the bright glowing lances flying across the street.

They didn't explode as they hit a wall. A loud buzz followed instead, along with a pungent but sweet scent. Irregular patches of different types of wood now lay scattered across the wall. Instant transmutation.

What the fuck would have happened if those had hit me?

Shay leapt to her feet, catching sight of the glowing witch as the woman hurried onto another side street. She holstered her weapon and now regretted driving around earlier in a car instead of a motorcycle or moped. A good tackle from a vehicle could end a fight quickly.

Loud static filled her earpiece. "Peyton, you still there?"

"Shay...I...losing..."

A massive wave of blue energy shot from the side street like a translucent tsunami.

This isn't good.

Shay winced and threw up her arms as the wave slammed into her. She blinked her eyes open after a few seconds.

"Huh, not dead. That's convenient." She sprinted toward the side street and skidded to a stop after she turned the corner and spotted her prey. The witch stood in the middle of the tree-lined street highlighted in an even brighter glow. The Scepter was pointed straight up.

A long moment passed during which the two women stared at each other before Shay realized the light *wasn't* brighter, but rather every other light in the area was off, making the glow seem stronger.

"Peyton?" she whispered. "Can you hear me?"

He didn't respond. There wasn't even any static over the link. She wasn't surprised, just annoyed.

Shay eyed the witch. "Magical EMP?"

"The Scepter of Dagobert responds to my will. You will *not* have it. You can't even harm me, so why do you insist on chasing me? I don't want to kill you, but I'll have no choice if you won't leave me alone."

"I'm a stubborn bitch, and I'm being paid. Sorry." Shay

shrugged and holstered her pistol. Her gun had already proven useless, but she trusted the adamantine knives to do the trick if she could close on the witch. "You've already admitted you can't control that thing like you want, and it's only going to get more dangerous. Just hand it over before you blow yourself and half this city up. You don't seem like a psycho. Do you really want to kill a bunch of people to prove some point to a bunch of mean girl witches or whatever?"

The witch gritted her teeth. "Don't...mock...me."

"Just saying."

The witch pointed the Scepter at a nearby tree. A blue bolt shot out and struck the trunk. Wood cracked as the plant pulled itself out of the ground, its roots replaced by spindly legs and its branches thrashing.

"Oh come on!" Shay sighed. "Guess that's what I get for not bringing my chainsaw."

"Do you understand now? I control so much power, and I will not surrender it to anyone."

"And you don't think this is a 'power corrupts' situation?"

The witch glared at Shay. "I don't believe anything you say. You just want to steal the Scepter of Dagobert from me. You're nothing more than a heartless mercenary."

"I prefer the term 'tomb raider' or 'field archaeologist,' but come on, chick. Use your head! There was a reason that thing was locked away for so many years."

The witch's lips pressed into a thin line, and she shook her head. "You'll have to kill me to take it, but it doesn't matter. There's no way you can win against me while I have it." She muttered something and made a few quick movements with the Scepter.

The tree lumbered toward the tomb raider, with no visible mouth, eyes, or weak spots.

Yeah, this is perfect. I miss the days when a tall guy with a gun was the weirdest thing I had to deal with on a job.

I've played nice, but it's time to end it.

Shay yanked a knife from a sheath and threw it at the other woman. It bounced off her with a blue flash but didn't vaporize like the bullets.

"Damn it."

"This is pathetic." The woman shook her head. "You thought you could win with a knife?"

Shay shrugged. "It's a very nice knife. A gnome made it for me."

She waited until the tree was nearly on her, then ducked underneath a striking branch and rushed the witch.

The witch flourished the wand in two swoops. A roar deafened Shay, and an invisible shockwave knocked her to the ground.

The walking tree got the worst of it, since the shockwave smashed into and reduced it to a shower of splinters and leaves. The old stones paving the side street cracked under the assault as well.

Shay crawled behind a nearby dumpster. She was coughing up blood, and every part of her body ached.

Why the fuck am I not dead? Huh. She keeps running, even with the wand. Maybe things are stronger for her far away. Time to bet my life on that.

Shay readied another knife, but a loud buzz sounded and the dumpster slammed into her. She grunted, and pain spiked in her arm. She rolled away from the dumpster and ignored the throbbing in her arm and the rest of the pain throughout her body.

Before, the increased illumination had been a trick of mere contrast, but there was no doubt now that the intensity of the glow around the woman had increased. Shay had to squint to even look directly at the witch.

What the fuck is going on? Is she getting stronger? Or maybe weaker?

The other woman took quick, ragged breaths as she gripped the Scepter with both hands, pointing it up at an angle.

"Why won't you die?" the witch shouted, this time in her native language.

"I told you before. I'm a stubborn bitch."

The witch whipped the Scepter down and Shay dodged a blue ball of energy that erupted from the wand. She closed on the woman, zigzagging to escape follow-up attacks.

Whatever the magical skills of the witch prior to finding the Scepter of Dagobert, it was painfully obvious she'd never been in a real fight. No anticipation, no leading of the target, no dynamic defense movements. The best weapon in the world meant nothing without proper training and experience.

Or killer instinct.

Shay closed the distance and brought her knife up. The witch's eyes widened as the tomb raider stabbed toward her heart.

"Got you."

The blade slammed into an invisible force, not even ripping the witch's dress.

"Shit," the tomb raider muttered. "That's just perfect. Fucking great."

The witch took a few steps back and looked down at her chest. She started laughing and lifted her wand. "I guess you lose, stubborn American bitch."

Shay spun and sprinted toward another open alley. Another harsh buzz filled the air a second before agonizing heat struck her back. She cried out and fell to the ground.

The tomb raider took a few deep breaths and threw off her jacket, or at least the burned tatters that remained of the leather.

The witch strode toward Shay with a wide grin on her face. The glow was even brighter now. It was as if a blue star had come to Earth, and two pulsing wings stretched from the woman's back.

Shay refused to close her eyes as the witch aimed the Scepter right at her head. Her pulse thundered in her ears.

"Just do it," the tomb raider shouted. "I'm not gonna beg."

The woman twitched and didn't respond.

"What's the matter, never kill anyone before?" Shay sneered. "If you're gonna try to play with the big girls, you have to…" She blinked as the woman collapsed to the ground, writhing and screaming.

Shay stood and slowly backed away from the woman, clueless about what the hell was going on.

The witch's limbs jerked and folded on themselves at painful angles, as if being rearranged by a sadistic invisible giant. Her blue wings grew longer and more solid, actual feathers sprouting into existence. The witch's shrill screams turned Shay's stomach. Intense light engulfed the woman, and Shay averted her gaze.

Nothing like being at Ground Zero in a massive magical explosion.

Shay let out a weary sigh and half-wished she could have at least gone out while eating some pizza. A bright blue flash enveloped her.

No heat. No new pain, only the lingering pain from before. No annoying noises.

Her eyes adjusted after a moment. The Scepter of Dagobert lay in the middle of the charred road, unmarred by even a scratch. A small bird covered in blue feathers tilted its head back and forth as it stared at Shay. She didn't know what type of bird it was, but it was hard to miss that it looked exactly like the top of the Scepter.

Shay snickered and remembered Tubal-Cain's words:

Be careful about misusing the artifact. Everything has consequences.

She grabbed the Scepter. "You need your own power before you can control other power." She gave a little wave to the bird, grabbed her knives off the ground, and struggled down the street, through the alleys and side streets until she reached her car. Street and building lights flickered on as she approached her vehicle.

Shay let out a sigh of relief. "Peyton, can you hear me?"

"Yeah. I can now, but I lost the drone."

"Lost the drone?"

"The feed's dead. I think the drone lost power and crashed. Last thing I saw was some weird flash from the witch."

"Yeah, there was some sort of EMP, but it's all over now, and I've got the Scepter. I'm driving straight to the airstrip and getting the hell out of the country."

"Nice. And the witch? You take her out?"

"Not exactly. Let's just say she's been given a second chance at life with a new perspective."

Shay yawned as she stepped down the stairs from the small plane, a large bag containing the Scepter in hand. Smite-Williams stood at the bottom, a large, thin silver case covered in runes lying on the ground next to him. It was large enough to fit the Scepter of Dagobert.

The Professor waited until she'd hit the ground to speak. "Did you have a good flight back, Miz Carson?"

She shrugged. "I mostly slept. Everything okay on your end? I know that job didn't go as quietly as you would have preferred."

"Aye. Although some people are well aware that something magical happened, they're attributing it to pranksters rather than something more serious. It's not like an entire building blew up." He chuckled.

"Only messed up some paving stones and a wall. Uh, and a tree." Shay opened the bag and handed him the Scepter. She didn't even want to touch the thing, but she didn't feel anything strange when she did.

Whether it was because she had no temptation to use such a dangerous object or her own lack of innate magical ability, she couldn't say.

She also didn't care. Magical artifacts had their uses,

but they were hard to trust. The witch's final fate had only reinforced that.

When Shay shot her gun, she knew it wouldn't turn her into a small animal if it took issue with her moral choices or used it too much.

The Professor's curious gaze roamed the Scepter for a half-minute before he knelt and stowed the powerful wand in the case. "We got lucky this time, and I wholeheartedly thank you for your assistance in this matter."

"You're welcome. And lucky? You mean we were lucky because she didn't blow up half of Paris?"

"Aye."

"Did you expect something like that?"

"Not necessarily."

Shay grimaced. "That's comforting."

"And that's the problem with powerful artifacts, Miz Carson. They can find their way into the hands of dangerous people."

Shay shrugged. "For what it's worth, I don't think she was evil, just power-tripping—not that I care she ended up turning into a bird. Bitch *did* try to kill me several times. If I weren't so badass, I'd be dead."

"A sad, misguided soul with a powerful artifact is as dangerous as a wicked one."

Shay smirked. "Now you really *do* sound like a priest, *Father O'Banion.*"

He shook his head. "Alas, I think my blood alcohol level has been allowed to reach zero. I should remedy that soon. The successful recovery of the Scepter of Dagobert is worth more than a few beers." He leaned over and narrowed his eyes. "Show me your back."

Shay turned. She hadn't bothered to change. The earlier blast had destroyed her jacket, but only scorched her shirt and skin.

"I've had worse," she pointed out. "Though it's going to make me invest in a few more healing potions."

"I think the injury is worth a bonus. You've earned it."

"That, and saving millions of people's lives?"

The Professor chuckled. "That was part of the main payment." He picked up the case. "Always a pleasure, Miz Carson, but I have to hand this over to some people."

"Sure thing, Professor."

Time to go home and take a long, well-deserved bath.

12

Peyton checked his hair in his rearview mirror one last time before stepping out into the parking lot, a smile on his face. Between Shay's French job and fighting off hackers probing the net, he' had no opportunities to follow up on any of his dating leads. Now, with a few free days and no threats, it was time to get his dating game on.

He sighed and looked down.

Is this a mistake? I mean, the last time I tried this it was a disaster, but here I am again, going out on a date with a woman who thinks I'm a random IT guy and not a research assistant for a tomb raider who used to be a killer and faked her own death.

Am I just setting myself up for pain?

He chuckled. How would women react if he added, "Faked my own death to escape a hitman" on his profile? All the advice sites always said a man should lead with his most interesting quality.

Maybe it's not a big deal. After all, everyone lies a little when they start dating. I just need her to not be as paranoid as Tricia was.

Peyton frowned.

Also need a better story. Avoid bullshit about tech start-ups or anything that'll lead to questions about stuff that's different from my normal day-to-day work. Just need to spin my normal job in a less obvious way.

This can work. I deserve it. I do a good job, and I don't want to date some strange criminal woman from Dante's or the Black Sun.

Peyton nodded to himself. He could do this, and there was no reason he shouldn't.

If Shay of all people gets to have a life complete with friends and a boyfriend, then I want that, too. Well, not a boyfriend, not even Captain Muscles Brownstone.

He slapped his cheeks to clear his head and headed toward the gastropub in a cocky strut. A pale, skinny woman with dark hair and dark glasses stood near the front, looking around. She stopped and focused on him.

Nice. Very nice.

It was Amber, his date. She looked exactly like her picture from the dating app, all the way down to the same navy-blue maxi dress.

Peyton had worn his powder blue suit for his most recent dating photos, but had gone for something a little more casual for this date: khaki shorts and a shirt that looked like a skull from a distance, but a closer examination revealed it was composed of several overlapping black and white images of cats.

He wasn't sure if it told people he was quirky or

psychotic. He knew what Shay would think but, he'd find out soon enough how a normal woman would react.

"Hey," Peyton offered. "Nice to finally meet you in person." He extended his hand.

Amber smiled and gave his hand a gentle shake. "Glad to see you're not some creeper who used a fake picture."

"The same."

Peyton stopped himself from wincing. It wasn't the smoothest line in the world.

Amber laughed. "You never know anymore."

"Yep."

"I mean, who does that, right? Like I wouldn't walk away if I show up to my date and find out that he's been lying. Being truthful is important in all..." She ran a hand through her hair. "Guess I'm babbling. I do that when I'm nervous."

"No, it's okay. I agree. I can't stand liars." He let out a little chuckle, hoping it didn't come off as nervous. "No reason to worry."

Yeah. Like lying about what I do for a living? Keep it together. This is just about having some fun, not trying to take her to Vegas tomorrow for a quickie wedding. Also, not going to try and rush things and take her home tonight.

This can work. I can have some fun if I don't overthink it.

Peyton hurried over to open the door for her. "Your table awaits, my lady."

"Thanks."

They headed inside and found an empty table. Light jazz played over the speakers at a reasonable volume. Only half the tables were filled, and the background chatter remained light. It made for good ambiance when combined with the music.

A waitress descended on them like a hawk as soon as they sat. After ordering a few cocktails, the two smiled across the table at each other.

"So," Peyton began, his hands folded in front of him, "you're a physicist. That's got to be interesting. Probing the fundamental mysteries of the universe and all that."

Amber laughed and waved a hand. "Oh, is that what you thought from my profile? I can see how it's confusing, but I don't want to misrepresent myself." She bit her lip. "Now I'm really embarrassed."

"You're not a physicist?"

"I…" The woman looked down. "Sorry."

"No, no. Not a big deal. It's not like I have some big impressive job. I'm just a computer guy. Great at my job, but still just a computer guy."

Amber looked up, hope in her eyes. "Same here. When I said I worked on computational physics, that's true. It's just that I don't do the research. I work with the physicists in the department who need help refining simulations for their work and developing custom simulation code for the scientists who are a little more clueless about programming in general."

Peyton nodded. "Sounds to me like you still have to know a lot about physics, though. It's not like they can give you a couple of lines about what they want, and you come up with a complicated simulation."

Scarlet spread on the woman's pale cheeks. "I guess that's true when you talk about it that way."

"Of course, it's true."

"What about you, Peyton? You mentioned computers before and on your profile, but you didn't talk about the kind of work." She let out a little laugh. "Are you working for some start-up? Are you going to be a billionaire in a few years?"

"No!" Peyton insisted.

Amber blinked at his vehemence.

Peyton gave her an apologetic smile. "Sorry, just really not into the whole start-up thing. I spend a lot of time doing research, and I develop specialty centers on natural language processing and filtering heuristics for autonomous internet research."

"That sounds interesting. I messed around with some of that in my undergraduate research, but it's not something I really have much need to do for the job I have now."

Peyton shrugged. "It can be interesting, but it's not like helping with physics research. I was reading the other day how the rise of magic resurrected string theory. Now everyone's saying it's the strongest chance we have, not only as a grand unification theory, but also as a magic and physics unification theory."

Amber nodded. "Yeah, one of the guys in my department is working on a unification theory centered around thirty-two dimensions."

"*Thirty-two* dimensions? I thought a lot of the string stuff centered around much lower numbers, like eleven." Peyton let out a nervous chuckle. "I'll be honest, though…a lot of that is way over my head. I read a book about Calabi-Yau manifolds, and I was glad I chose to go into computers instead of physics."

"Most people don't even know what a Calabi-Yau manifold is."

"I'm still not sure I do, other than a bunch of dimensions folded up."

"Kind of." Amber shrugged. "But that solution was to explain things before magic. Now a lot of scientists are focusing on magical and normal physics unification. It's exciting because now they have a whole new frontier to understand."

"I can imagine. People used to talk about how we were at the edge of new discovery, and now we know there's so much more out there."

Amber grinned. "Exactly. After all, you can't claim you understand the fundamental structure of the universe and then ignore the fact that you have witches and elves running around casting spells." She slapped a hand on the table, her face alight with excitement. "Kind of like this project I worked on."

"I'd love to hear about it."

"I helped the guy in my department with some simulations last year that suggested that you can account for the effects of some types of magic via lower-order strings that are way shorter than Planck Length. Some of the topological spaces he's proposing make Calabi-Yau manifolds look like something a five-year-old thought up."

"A damned smart five-year-old."

Amber laughed.

Peyton allowed himself a cocky grin. Things were going well. Very well. "So magic is just physics that hasn't been explained?"

"Sure. It's not like it's that random. It still seems to obey rules and has limits and that sort of thing, even if the rules are kind of weird sometimes. Just because it breaks the rules of the physics we know doesn't make it that mysterious. Many branches of physics are weird, like quantum mechanics, and they seemed almost beyond reason at first."

The waitress arrived with their cocktails. They thanked her, and both took a few sips before continuing their conversation.

Peyton rubbed his chin. "Yeah, I guess it's like Newtonian physics was true enough for what we could see and experience, and then with relativity and quantum mechanics, we realized what we thought we understood wasn't the case. They explain stuff that we're just not used to encountering on a daily basis, so it's hard to wrap our minds around it. Our common sense fails us.

"Now, we have a whole planet of people coming with things that they take for granted, but we always thought were kid's stories."

"Exactly!" Amber looked down, her cheeks reddening.

Peyton gave a look of concern. "What's wrong?"

"Sorry. Didn't mean to get geek out so much."

"I'm wearing a cat-skull shirt. I'm more on the geek side than anything."

Amber laughed. "I like the shirt."

"Thanks."

She sighed. "I just really like this sort of thing. I talk to people at work about it, but it's hard to find people outside the department who want to talk about it, and it doesn't help that I double-majored in physics and CS back in college. I only didn't go into physics because I'm just not that creative."

"I find that hard to believe."

Woah. I wasn't even trying to be smooth, but that was totally smooth. Good job, me!

Amber smiled softly. "The problem is I kind of need to have a concrete problem set in front of me, and then I can go about solving it. I'm not a good theorist."

"Not every scientist is a good theorist. Just think of yourself as an experimentalist." Peyton shrugged. "I'm the same way." He took another sip of his drink. "But don't you think that's where creativity can shine?"

"What do you mean?"

"If it were so easy to do what you do, all those physicists would be able to do it, and you'd be out of a job." He reached over and put his hand atop hers. "You're applying creativity to problem-solving. That's the way I look at it." Peyton removed his hand and leaned back in his chair, not sure if he was relaxed because of the booze or because of how well the conversation was unfolding. "I've always been good with computers. It may sound arrogant, but I'm a natural. I develop new algorithms and techniques all the time. *I* think it's creative, and I'm helping push knowledge by using those creatively developed tools, even if I'm not the guy actually thinking up what questions to ask."

Amber stared at Peyton, wide-eyed. "Just...wow. I can't believe this."

"What?"

Peyton's stomach tightened. Had he screwed up somewhere? Did he sound too arrogant?

"Most of the time I go out with guys and start talking about this sort of thing, and their eyes glaze over. If it's not the computers, it's the physics."

"I consider myself a bit of a Renaissance Man." Peyton winced. "Did I just sound like a douchebag? Be honest."

Amber let out a quiet laugh. "I don't think so. I think you're pretty interesting." She shrugged. "And cute."

Wow. This date is going better than I could have possibly imagined.

———

Peyton finished off his spicy chicken wing and set it on the growing pile of remnants on his plate. "I never even thought to modify the algorithm that way. That's brilliant. I can save tons of time on a lot of data processing if I implement that."

Amber beamed. "I'd like to say that I thought it up, but to be honest, I made a mistake in the code and it just happened to work better."

"Hey, I'm not the person to complain about a lucky accident. They've gotten me this far."

A comfortable silence descended upon the pair as they finished off their food.

Things are going super-well. Sure, I'm not exactly being a hundred percent honest about who I work for, but everything else I've said is true. And it's not like she's asking me a bunch of questions I'm having to lie about, so that's a good thing, I think.

She seems to be into me, and she's cute and smart, and she doesn't look like the kind of woman who will threaten me with a gun if I piss her off.

"What are you thinking about?" Amber asked, her voice soft.

"About the importance of honesty." He winked.

Amber smiled as they stepped through the front door of the gastropub. She pointed in the distance. "Well, that's my car. I should get going."

What does that mean? Did she have a good time, or didn't she? Guess I should check.

Peyton leaned in for a kiss, but she turned her cheek and hugged him. He hugged her back.

Is this a good sign or a bad sign?

Amber released him and waved. "See you around."

"See you around."

Peyton could finally move his feet once the woman pulled out of the parking lot. He was still unsure if he'd had the most awesome date of his entire life or crashed and burned.

Peyton rested his hands on the back of his head as he stared up at the night's sky sitting in a lawn chair set up on the beach. The bright lights of LA pushed a dome of illumination into the night sky. Osiris rested on his chest.

"Man looked up at the stars and wondered for so many years, and now we're slowly blocking them, even at night. I read the other day that there are cities on Earth now where people can't see a single star at night."

Osiris meowed.

"Yeah, you're right. I shouldn't worry about that. I should figure out how I might make things work with Amber. She's definitely my type." Peyton tilted his head up to where several pops of light were shooting overhead and toward the ocean. "Those make me think about aliens, you know, Osiris? I know they're real now. Maybe a lot of them are. Oriceran is one thing, but what if the entire galaxy is teeming with life?"

Several more pops of light flew overhead, and loud booms echoed. Osiris hopped off Peyton's chest and hissed. This sort of thing had become far too common lately.

Peyton sighed and rolled his eyes. "Magic returns to Earth, and what do we get? Assholes using their wands to annoy people. Great. Thugs with wands. The aliens would probably just be thugs with spaceships."

13

S hay sighed as she looked at the sign taped to the front window of the gated store. She recognized Tubal-Cain's atrocious handwriting.

Due to employee vacations, Prophecy Gaming will be closed for a few days.

Not that the average person could even perceive the store to enter it. Who was the sign even *for*? Her?

Shay ran a hand down her face and let out a loud groan. The gnome's aversion to using a cell phone always made getting hold of him an adventure. His recent trips out of town were making it downright annoying. It was almost like he knew she had the information and was purposefully avoiding her.

No, that's not it. The guy thinks it's going to take me months to find his cousin. Just bad luck, but I really could use those magical lockpicks. Could make my next job way easier.

The average human had absorbed the collective wisdom concerning security based on centuries of technology. Locks, walls, gates. Guards with guns. Magical security? Not so much.

Earth would catch up, but in the interim, there were a lot of opportunities for a woman to perform a little mischief with magic.

Shay shrugged and rejoined the flow of people passing by the shop and not paying it any heed.

Wait too long, and your cousin might move again. Don't blame me.

Wealthy people were smarter, better, and more knowledgeable. They deserved everything they had. Luck wasn't a factor. That was what many people assumed, particularly the wealthy themselves.

Marcus opened the jewelry box and smiled down at the sparkling diamond necklace inside. He understood that the rich were nothing more than people with money, and because they overestimated themselves, their arrogance blinded them and made them the perfect targets for a skilled practitioner of the fine art of burglary.

This looks even more expensive than I expected. Guess I'm just lucky.

A six-figure necklace shouldn't have been sitting in a jewelry box in a mansion with no guards and a security system that didn't include alarmed second-story windows.

People that arrogant need to be humbled. This is a good lesson for them. An expensive lesson, but still a good one. Hell, I've been humbled tons of times, and it's only made me better.

The thief chuckled to himself and slipped the necklace

into a plastic bag before placing it in his backpack.

"Too damned easy. I'm almost disappointed."

Marcus strode over to the open window and the rope stretching from the window to a nearby rooftop of a huge abandoned tire warehouse. The nice home was separated from an industrial zone by a mere fence, the glamour of the neighborhood long faded into the past. The mansion was the last redoubt of a lost way of life.

Maybe that was why the couple obsessed over expensive jewelry? Marcus didn't know, even if he liked to ponder the psychology of his victims on occasion.

He climbed out hand-over-hand, whistling to himself. An easy job was welcome, and the money would keep him in drinks at some tropical paradise for a long time, but he'd been expecting at least a minor challenge. Mastering skills was pointless if you never got to use them.

As Marcus arrived at the other end of his rope, a loud alarm howled from the house.

"Oh, that's more like it."

He pulled out a knife and cut the rope with one swift stroke. He wanted a challenge, but he didn't want to make it too easy for anyone who might pursue him, either.

You probably want a challenge too, even if you don't know it.

A smile on his face, the cat burglar charged toward the edge of his current rooftop and leapt to the next.

Shay moaned and let her head loll back. She loved history and archaeology, but that didn't mean she enjoyed every presentation related to those subjects.

An Analysis of Pre-Twenty-First Century Contact With Oricerans: A Modern Cross-Disciplinary Approach was a dry book. Dry as the Sahara Desert. No, not even that. Dry as fucking *Mercury*.

Any sort of narrative style designed to make the information more digestible had been eschewed in favor of maximum density. The nested footnotes didn't help things. At least a reader could never claim they didn't know where the authors had gotten their information.

The tomb raider wanted to stick the book back on the shelf, but every time she was about to give up, some interesting tidbit popped up that drew her back in. The back of her neck tingled as if she were about to stumble upon some critical fact. Whether that was instinct or wishful thinking was up for debate.

Okay, I can do this. It's why I came to Warehouse Four tonight anyway.

Today's subject of interest was Correk. She still didn't know a lot about the man, and her typical methods of gaining information were running into dead ends or strange anecdotes that obviously had nothing to do with the Light Elf.

A little digging netted an off-hand reference in some chef's memoir about a Renaissance Faire actor going by that name in Austin, Texas over twenty years prior. Shay chalked that up to weird coincidence. She was sure that if she pushed hard enough, she could probably find a dark-haired woman named Shay in Texas regardless of the year.

I need to figure out more about this guy. Something about him is bothering me. My gut tells me he's a lot more than just some Elf Mafia collector, and way more dangerous.

Shay looked back down at her book and its painfully detailed discussion about the Light Elf language and its musical qualities.

An alarm sounded on her phone, and she picked it from the table.

PERIMETER ALERT, WAREHOUSE FOUR. MOTION AND CONTACT ALARMS 1 AND 3 TRIPPED AT 21:22.

Shay narrowed her eyes and brought up her security app. Peyton's customizations had made controlling security at the warehouses easier—a perfect gift for the paranoid woman in a man's life.

Thanks, Peyton.

"Where the fuck is the…"

A loud thud from the roof echoed through the warehouse. The source impact knocked down years of accumulated dust from part of the ceiling in a thick cloud that descended toward one of her bookshelves.

Shay winced.

"Okay, asshole, I don't know if you followed me or you're just picking a place at random, but now I'm ready to give you a beat-down. No one messes with my library."

Shay examined a camera feed from her phone. A dark-haired, dark-clothed man wearing a backpack knelt near the edge of the roof of the warehouse. He reached into his backpack and pulled out a small plastic bag.

"That's an expensive-ass necklace." Shay burst out laughing. "Oh, bet it's from the Blackwell place. They should have moved a long time ago. Wait, what the fuck is he doing?"

The thief returned the plastic bag to his backpack, sat

down cross-legged, and pulled out an apple. He took a bite, with a smile on his face like he had all the time in the world to enjoy his rooftop picnic.

"You arrogant prick, you're not that far from the place you probably just robbed. The cops could still tag you with a drone. Shit."

Shay snatched her gun from the table and rushed toward the door. She needed this asshole away from Warehouse Four before any private security or police came snooping. There was no way she could evacuate this place quickly, even with the help of Purity Solutions.

Her heart pounding, she made it outside in record time and up a ladder to the roof so fast she couldn't even remember the climb when she finished it. She sprinted toward the man chomping away on fruit in the center of the roof, illuminated by the dim light of the stars and street lights a few buildings away.

The thief hopped to his feet and tilted his head, a curious look on his face.

He bowed with a flourish. "It truly is my lucky night."

"I don't know about that, asshole."

He laughed. "Such a beautiful woman shouldn't use such foul language." His gaze dipped.

What, he's checking me out now? Seriously? Does he even get the situation?

"And use such awful weapons," the thief commented.

Shay snorted. She wasn't wearing a jacket, and her shoulder holster was visible.

Good, he knows I'm dangerous. That might make this much easier.

Shay glared at the cat burglar. "You picked the wrong

night to piss me off."

He saluted. "Oh, I see. You're some sort of champion of justice, disappointed in a man who is just trying to make his way in the world."

"I'm no champion of justice, and did anyone ever tell you that you're really fucking annoying?"

He grinned. "Many, many times."

Screw this.

Shay charged him. If he wasn't going to pull a gun, then she only needed to get him moving away from Warehouse Four, or she could knock his ass out and drag him away. Whatever worked.

The thief sprinted toward the side of the roof.

Idiot. What are you going to do, flap your arms and fly away?

He reached the edge and jumped. Shay blinked and slowed. The man sailed through the air and landed on the next roof over without even a grunt and rolled back to his feet in seconds.

"Okay, that was impressive, but now it's on, asshole." The whole thing reminded her of something she'd seen Lily do a hundred times at least. Lily or one of the teenagers from beneath the ground. She put it out of her head and focused.

Shay backed up and charged the edge of the roof and pushed off. Unlike the other man she didn't manage a roll, causing the full force of her leap to rocket up her legs.

She hissed as the cat burglar sped away.

"Not getting away that easily." Shay pumped her legs and sprinted after the man.

The milder height differences between the next few

roofs helped reduce the impact, but the slippery bastard in front of her maintained his distance.

A few roofs later he jumped out, arms first, legs down.

Shay stopped at the edge, convinced he was about to break both his legs. He fell at an angle and grabbed the edge of a window before pushing off and hitting the wall of the first building with his legs. The thief maintained his momentum and continued bouncing between the walls until he was on the ground.

The tomb raider jumped and grabbed a nearby drainpipe. She shinnied down the pipe as the thief sat grinning like it was the most entertaining sight in the world.

I'm so going to put my foot up his ass.

Two rusty screws pulled out of the top, and the pipe ripped away from the wall.

"Shit!"

Shay dropped to the ground with a grunt. The man was already running. The tomb raider gritted her teeth and sprinted after him, her heart thundering and her lungs burning.

The thief grabbed the handrail on a metal staircase and vaulted onto the stairs. A series of similar movements on the rails on other side had him halfway up before Shay even got to the bottom. She tried to replicate his move and almost sent herself over the edge.

Shay had stamina, as well as grip and muscle strength. She trained every day in Warehouse One when she was in LA, but she could barely keep up with this asshole master of momentum.

A loud groan ripped from her mouth as she crested the stairs and saw the man jump to a flagpole, swinging around a few times before sliding down. It finally dawned on her what she was dealing with.

Parkour, French-invented mobility training. Half-sport, half-non-combat martial art.

"Damn it."

Shay hurried to the edge of the building and leapt for the flagpole. She didn't manage the smooth connection of the parkour master and slid halfway before arresting her fall with her feet and the crook of her arm.

She dropped off the pole. At least they were both on the ground now.

The tomb raider burst into a sprint, ignoring the ache building in her legs and her ragged breathing. This wasn't about scaring the man away from Warehouse Four anymore. This was about proving to herself that some random asshole who had hopped onto her roof wasn't better than her.

I'm the best. I'm gonna tackle his ass, tie him up, stick that necklace on his neck, and call the cops on him.

The thief ran straight up a car and leapt from the roof to the hood of the next one. Shay closed on him and stomped over the same car.

Hope you have insurance for those dents.

The pair passed over a half-dozen cars parked in a line on the street. She'd gained a yard on him, but he was still out of reach. Several people along the street stopped and watched them.

A tall metal fence blocked the path ahead and Shay picked up her pace, hoping to close before the man made it over.

He hopped into the air and pushed with his arms. His

body twisted, and he vaulted over the fence, spinning a few times before landing.

Shay didn't even bother to try and replicate the move. She scrambled up the fence in a far less elegant manner, losing valuable seconds as the man continued running.

Sweat poured down her face as she pushed her heart and lungs to her limit. So close. So damned close. She would win. She *had* to win.

The thief changed directions and ran straight toward a park bench. The move confused Shay since there were an alley and stairs in the opposite direction.

Shay allowed herself a grin. The man had finally made a mistake.

He reached the bench and used it to launch himself into the air toward a busy street. He landed atop a metro bus zooming down the street, then sat up and saluted Shay, a shit-eating grin on his face.

Shay stood there watching as the bus pulled away, the driver oblivious to the cat burglar now riding for free.

"Damn it!" she screamed into the night.

All her training, all her experience, and she'd been beaten. She'd never even gotten close to the guy.

She huffed and wiped the sweat off her face. The man's face as he rode away remained etched in her mind. He didn't even look that winded.

"Next time, asshole. Next time."

Shay dropped onto the park bench the man had used for his final escape. "Maybe I need to learn a little parkour."

She sighed.

First, though, she had a little more dry-ass reading to finish.

"Ah, good afternoon, Miz Carson," answered the cheerful voice of Smite-Williams over the phone. "It's rare that you contact me instead of the other way around."

"I need to meet with Correk."

"He doesn't offer general assignments."

Shay sucked in a breath. After her little fun episode with the cat burglar, she'd thought it'd be even harder to return to research, but a chance passage in her first book had led to her spending hours reading others. She now had a good idea of Correk's true identity, and she needed to confirm it.

Think I would have liked it more if you were just Elf Mafia.

"Are you saying you won't pass my message along, Professor?"

"I don't mean to be difficult, but I value my relationship with him, so I need to know why I should."

"Because he's interested in that alien shit as much as I

am, and it might be in his best interest to deal with me directly."

"I see." The Professor let out a long sigh. "I'll pass along your message, but I can't guarantee anything."

"Fine by me."

He made me come all the way to fucking DC? Why? He doesn't know how to use a phone?

Shay marched up the steps of the Lincoln Memorial, muttering about inconvenience as she crested them. The mammoth white marble statue of Abraham Lincoln was, as always, seated and eternally looking forward.

I bet someday some wizard will enchant that statue and have him go on a rampage. Honest Abe kicking ass and taking names.

The tomb raider stepped between two of the Doric columns dominating the front of the memorial and looked around for her contact. Correk hadn't been all that clear about where he'd be, other than offering the time and telling her to meet him "somewhere" at the memorial.

"Miz Carson," called a familiar voice.

Shay spun around, her hand going into her purse toward her gun.

Correk stood, his arms crossed, in front of one of the columns. He had a thin smile on his face.

Shay let her hand drop and walked toward him. "This isn't exactly a private place, and I want to discuss private things. I thought the Professor would have made that clear."

DEAD IN PLAIN SIGHT

Correk nodded toward a gaggle of school kids strolling past. "Notice anything?"

The tomb raider narrowed her eyes and looked for any sign of danger from the kids—suspicious bulges, strange tricks of the light, anything unusual—but they just looked like a mass of kids walking toward Abraham Lincoln. They chatted, smiling and laughing.

She blinked. She couldn't hear any of it.

"So they can't hear us," Shay commented. "Can they see us?"

"Not if we don't give them a reason to."

Shay shook her head. "Still seems dangerous."

"Oh, not as much as you expect, but it's only because of Smite-Williams' recommendation that I even agreed to meet with you alone. You're obviously resourceful, and I'm curious what you want to talk to me about."

Shay took a deep breath. She'd have to risk giving up information at the chance of gaining information. Trusting some Light Elf she barely knew, even if he was a friend of the Professor, still knotted her stomach, but she could no longer keep operating as if she could solve every problem by herself.

Peyton and James had both shown her what she could accomplish when she dared to allow someone to help her.

She also needed contacts, and not just the Professor and a few others interested in artifacts. A woman with magical enemies needed magical allies.

"We discussed some of this before," Shay explained. "But to get it all out on the table, I'm aware of at least three stones with alien writing, including the one I recovered in

Illinois, and another artifact also with alien writing, but *different* alien writing."

Correk arched a brow. "*Different* alien writing?"

"I'm saying it's not from Earth or Oriceran, but it's different from what you were interested in before. Maybe the same planet, or maybe a different planet entirely. The writing is associated with an artifact of impressive power."

"Care to elaborate?"

Shay shook her head. "There's only so much I'm at liberty to share."

The corners of Correk's mouth turned up in a faint smile. Something approaching approval appeared in his eyes.

"So," the Light Elf replied, "do you know anything else?"

"Some associates of mine have been able to translate at least part of a message on the stones."

"Interesting. Very interesting. And are you at liberty to share that?"

Shay shrugged. "All they could figure out was, 'Already here.'"

"Already here?" Correk echoed. "That could mean a lot of things. It could mean something like, 'Don't come to Earth, the magic is already here, and it's too dangerous,' or it could mean something like, 'All our forces are already here and ready to invade.'"

"Yeah, it could. Not claiming I know what the total message says." She frowned. "So I've given you some info. Now I want some in return."

"I'm under no obligation to give you anything. How do I know I can even trust you?"

Shay snorted. "Because I risked my life to grab the

Scepter of Dagobert and deliver it to the Professor instead of selling it to whatever sketchy asshole would pay the most."

Correk's eyes narrowed.

The tomb raider smirked. "Yeah, I bet you were involved in that behind the scenes. I almost know you were."

The elf didn't speak. Instead, he turned and watched the silent crowds flow past with a distant look in his eye.

"What do you want from me, Miz Carson?"

"I want to know something I don't already know."

Correk gave a small nod. "Show me the pictures. All the symbols you have."

Shay locked eyes with him. For all she knew, the Light Elf had some sort of total recall spell. The minute she showed him the symbols, she'd lost a lot of her leverage. She did have a stone, but she wasn't sure if it had power, and it wasn't like she could trade Brownstone's amulet.

"Fine," she spat, reaching into her purse. Shay pulled out her phone and brought up the photo containing all the stones and a close-up of the amulet.

Correk stroked his chin as he looked over the symbols. "These aren't from Earth."

"No shit." Shay rolled her eyes. "Thanks for nothing."

He held up a hand. "But I've seen them before, and I don't mean on the stone you recovered for the Professor."

Shay slipped her phone back into her purse. "Oh?"

"I've seen them on Oriceran, but they aren't Oriceran. I assumed they were from Earth, but your research, among other information I have seen, points to the fact that they aren't." He furrowed his brow. "And this is troublesome."

"Why? Does this involve some sleeping alien god or something?"

"Maybe."

Shay blinked. "Maybe?"

"I'll be honest—I don't know yet. Many odd things have happened on Oriceran throughout the millennia that can't be explained, even with appeals to magic. When odd things have happened on Earth it's been easy to assume that someone from Oriceran was responsible, but the converse is a bit more difficult to justify."

"So you're saying E.T. showed up not just on Earth but on Oriceran?"

"'E.T.?'"

"Yeah, like, E.T. the Extraterrestrial from the old movie."

Correk shrugged. "Haven't seen it."

Shay smirked. "Bet you haven't seen a lot of movies."

"You might be surprised, but that's beside the point. You've stumbled upon something important, but there's a more pressing question here. Why should I tell you anything more about this?"

"Not impressed by my super-wand recovery?"

Correk chuckled. "Not enough. You gave me some information, and I've given you some information, but that doesn't mean I trust you, nor should you trust me."

Shay ran her tongue inside her cheek as she thought that over. "I've been doing a lot of reading lately."

"Always a good hobby."

Guess it's time to drop the bomb on him and see how he reacts.

"And it's led me to some interesting things. Things you might find interesting."

Correk leaned against the column and crossed his arms. "Such as?"

"A very important being known as the Fixer."

"Oh? Isn't that a criminal who helps criminals find things or something like that?" Correk grinned. "It's hard to keep track of human culture at times, let alone American culture."

Shay shrugged. "It's just kind of funny."

"I agree. Human culture is often amusing."

"No, it's just there's a similar title for Light Elves." She held up a hand. "I know, I know. It's some ridiculous music-sounding thing, but translated, it's 'the Fixer.'"

"Oh? Do tell."

Shay gave the Light Elf a feral grin. It was time to prove she wasn't just a badass.

"The Fixer is a Light Elf chosen about every eight to nine hundred years. The Fixer has access to a library of spell books and books on magic."

"A lot of elves have access to spell books and books on magic. What's so special about the Fixer?"

"Yeah, but this isn't a normal library. The whole point is this Fixer has special access to special knowledge, things the average Light Elf or even the average magical being won't have access to."

Correk uncrossed his arms. "And what does this Fixer do with it?"

"Help magical beings on Earth. Not just Light Elves, but *all* magical beings." Shay chuckled, her mercenary heart making it hard to get the words out. "It's an honored position and very respected. Revered, even, by people in the know in the magical community. There has been a Fixer on Earth for thousands of years. Maybe longer."

"What a fascinating tale. Very educational. And what does it have to do with me?"

Shay took a deep breath. Time to cross the Rubicon. "The Fixer was Turner Underwood." She laughed. "Which explains a lot about the School of Necessary Magic, but you are now the Fixer. Both Light Elves."

Correk stared at her, his expression unreadable for what felt like an agonizing eternity before he raised a brow. "Impressive, Miz Carson. I'll be honest—you're more resourceful than I gave you credit for."

"A lot of people underestimate me. Don't feel too bad."

"You already know my background." He pushed off the column, all the ease gone from his stance. "I did **my** homework, too."

Shay smirked. "Did you now? What did you find out?"

"For one thing, you're looking rather well for a dead woman."

Shay's jaw tightened.

Correk gave a broad smile. "But I can see why you'd want to leave such a vicious and self-serving life behind, and you were right about the Scepter. You've gathered several dangerous artifacts and could have passed them along to less than scrupulous people, but you've kept your word."

"Don't get me wrong...I'm not a good person. I just believe in the value of maintaining positive relationships that lead to mutual benefit."

Correk let out a weary sigh. "I'm far, far older than you

and I've dealt with evil you couldn't possibly imagine, so excuse me if I'm not overly impressed by your jaded act. So what's it to be, Miz Carson?"

"Nothing special. I just want to know more about the alien stones. It's both a professional and personal matter. I figure we can swap information."

"I can see value in us working together." Correk turned and stepped away.

"Where you going?"

"We both now know where we're coming from and what the other knows, and someone is waiting for me." The elf waved. "When you get in your car, you'll see that my number is in your phone."

The silence gripping their small slice of the Lincoln Memorial vanished, and the chatter of tourists and excited school children broke over Shay. Correk walked down the steps, his hands in his pockets.

The Professor acts like he knows my background too, but he keeps working with me. This might bite him and his elf buddy in the ass in the end. I'm not the good person they seem to think I am.

Shay waited until Correk had disappeared into the nearby crowds to make her way down the steps and back toward the parking lot and her rental car.

Hanging around a guy like Correk might get me targeted by some dangerous assholes. Maybe it's not worth it.

Shay spun, a frown on her face. She couldn't shake the feeling of someone's eyes on her. There were plenty of people on the street, but no one she could pick out as a spy. She sighed and turned back around. A quick check under the car didn't reveal any evidence of tampering or explosives. Everything looked fine.

She pulled off her purse and set it on the passenger seat. It fell over, and a tiny ball of light rolled onto the seat. She reached into the car to grab the ball.

"Son of a bitch. Is this a tracking spell?"

Shay snatched her phone and checked her contacts list. There was a new entry: NOT UNDERWOOD.

She snorted and texted the number.

I saw your little light. Not smooth, dude.

Her phone chimed seconds later with a response.

Just seeing if you were paying attention. Have a nice day.

The ball popped in her hand.

Shay groaned. "Elves."

15

Shay drummed her fingers on her leg. She didn't like being in the passenger seat, even with her friend Bella's nice leather seats. A lack of control never sat well with her, but she'd screwed up before by driving very nice vehicles. Now she just never let her friends see her in anything fancy. She was supposed to be a humble professor, not a globe-trotting adventurer who earned millions per job. It was the details that blew a false identity.

She stared out the windows. It was nice to spend a night with her girlfriends after all the craziness in recent weeks. This would just be a good dinner with friends, no crazy witches with powerful wands or mysterious elves. No gunning down hundreds of cartel douchebags, either—not that she hadn't enjoyed the last.

Shay frowned, tension suffusing her body. They were damned close to Warehouse Three.

This is stupid. I have no reason to worry about that. A lot of places in LA are close to a warehouse. I've got five of the damned things, after all.

"Where were we going again?" she inquired, keeping her tone casual.

"A modern Italian fusion place called Bestia," Janelle chimed in from the back.

"Italian, huh?"

Maybe I should make James take me to a nice Italian place. That shouldn't be too weird for him to handle. It's not super-exotic, and there'll be plenty of meat, even if it isn't barbeque. The man needs to broaden his horizons.

"I wish we hadn't gone this way," Kara commented, rubbing her shoulders.

Bella frowned. "Why? This is the quickest way to get to the restaurant, according to my GPS."

"Yeah, I know. My office isn't that far from here, and my carpool often drives this way."

Shay looked over her shoulder at her friend. "So? What's the big deal?"

Kara looked down. "It's just... I think there's a haunted building on the route."

Janelle, Bella, and Shay laughed.

Kara sighed. "There's this weird old building about two blocks down. It's some sort of old warehouse, but I don't think it's used for that anymore. Sometimes I hear the strangest things when going by it, even from the car."

Shit. Of course, she had to notice Warehouse Three.

"Maybe they shoot porn there," Shay suggested.

Everyone laughed, and the tension melted off Kara's face. Shay kept a smile plastered on her face.

Shoot something there.

Shay downed some Spaghetti Rustichella, enjoying the citrus notes and sweetness of the Dungeness Crab as her friends chattered. It'd been a while since she'd had good Italian.

At her insistence, the group had been seated at a table in the rear. Shay sat with her back toward the wall, giving her a full view of the dining room. It was a perfect defensive seating arrangement. She hadn't announced to her friends that she had a 9mm pistol sitting in her purse, but even if they found out it wouldn't be a huge deal. People packing heat in LA weren't rare.

The adamantine knife might be more difficult to explain. Shay smirked at the thought.

Her eyes flicked to the side at some quick movement. No assassin with a knife or gun was there, only a waiter, wiping his brow in relief at catching a plate that had fallen. Another sweep of the front revealed only a room filled with well-dressed people enjoying their meals.

Young, old, men, women, different races, and even a few elves in the far corner. It was like most places in LA—a cross-section of modern America.

Situational alertness wasn't a bad skill to practice, and her encounter with Correk had only reinforced that no matter how far she ran from her past, she couldn't be sure someone wouldn't dig it up and come looking.

Her original plan to stockpile money and hide in some

tropical paradise far from urban civilization didn't seem so bad in retrospect.

She resisted sighing. The plan hadn't seemed so bad before because she'd had nothing holding her back, but now she did: James and Alison. Hell, even Peyton and her girlfriends.

Friends and family. Still can't tell if they are making me better or weaker.

Bella smiled at Kara. "So, how is everything going with your guy? Didn't know if this was a burning-through-quickly kind of thing or the start of something more. You've been spending a lot of time with him."

Kara shrugged. "It's going great. The sex is great, but I don't know. We're still in that initial stage where everything feels good, and we're ignoring each other's flaws. I don't know yet if this is going to be something long-term."

"It doesn't have to be. Just have fun, and if it grows into something more, then it does."

Janelle sipped some wine and nodded. "I had to kick Darius to the curb in the end, but I can't say I regretted our time together. It was fun for a while."

Shay resisted a smirk. She'd had a confrontation with Janelle's ex-boyfriend to keep him from harassing her friend, though the more time she spent around her friend, the less convinced she was that the woman couldn't have handled it.

"So, any plans now?" she asked.

Janelle shook her head. "Nope. I think I'm just going to spend some time rediscovering who I am." She offered Shay a sly grin. "And so when were you planning on telling us about your man?"

The other two women's eyes widened, and they leaned in to stare at Shay.

"You bitch," Bella offered with a laugh. "You snagged a guy, and you didn't even tell us."

Kara nodded her agreement.

Shay blinked and looked between the three women, her fingers tightening around her fork. There was no way Janelle could have known about James. Even though Shay had briefly discussed him absent any real details before, she'd never shown them any pictures or talked about him after that.

Dark scenarios ran through the tomb raider's mind, with Janelle as a spy or a cat's paw of Yulia or even Correk.

Wait, that doesn't even make sense. The timing would be too weird unless...

"How..." Shay began. She sighed.

Admitting she was in a relationship shouldn't be such a big deal. If they insisted on meeting James, she could always just make up an excuse. Telling the truth wasn't an option, given how famous the bounty hunter had grown.

I'm trying to hide in the shadows, and he's showing up on the news. Interesting pair we make.

Shay gulped down some wine under the careful gaze of her three friends. "How did you know?"

Janelle smirked and leaned back. "I can just see it. You've always been so tense. I think you need to switch jobs, because all that archaeology is going to give you a heart attack."

"You don't know the half of it."

"Exactly, but now you're not as tense, which means two things: You've got a man, and you're getting some."

All the women laughed.

Not as tense, even though I've been searching the room for threats?

Shay finished her wine, the pleasant buzz slicing away some of the paranoia. "Okay, I admit that I've got a new guy, but you were all wrong. That's one of the reasons I didn't want to say anything."

Bella tilted her head. "We were all wrong?"

"I told you about the guy, but everyone said he was gay."

"Oh, *that* guy."

The three other women exchanged looks and grins.

"Why don't you tell us a little about him?" Janelle prodded.

"He's a really private guy," Shay offered. "I think he'd be annoyed if I talked about him too much. He's not all that used to relationships. He's been career-focused most of his life. His whole life is his job, barbeque, and this girl he's adopting."

Shit, that's probably too much information.

"Wow, a family man already," Kara commented.

Janelle looked thoughtful. "Be careful. Those career guys don't always know what they really want from life. They play around, but don't want to commit. Just because he's got a kid doesn't mean he'll commit to you."

Shay chuckled. "I'm not sure *I* know what I really want from life."

Janelle smirked. "You do what you need to do, girl. Just make sure you're running things."

Am I running things? I don't know. James isn't exactly clued into a lot of this stuff. I had to practically throw myself at him to get his attention, but it's also not like he's staring at other women and waiting for his chance to step out, either.

"I am really happy for you," Bella offered. "I've been so worried about you working too hard. I know you're an archaeologist and everything, but the future is always more important than the past."

Shay chuckled and refilled her wine glass. Not all that long ago she might not have believed that, but now she wasn't so sure. Things were starting to change, albeit slowly.

The women lapsed into reflective silence as they continued to sip their wine and attend to what was left of their entrées. The varied conversations of the nearby tables flowed over and around them.

Shay took the opportunity to survey the restaurant again. Her attention lingered on a few men in a booth on the opposite end of the room, but their rowdy, drunken laughter made it unlikely they were hitmen trying to sneak in a hit.

A couple of waiters emerged from the back. She focused on them to ensure they were staff she'd seen already that night. Dressing as waitstaff and shooting someone was something she'd done more than a few times.

Spun right from dating to looking for enemies.

The tomb raider forced down the laugh that wanted to erupt. Chatting with her friends and being personal without giving them the truth had become easier as the months had passed. Compartmentalizing her life had become normal.

Could I have had friends even back as a killer? Maybe not.

I'm not going to kid myself. The edge is still there, but it's not as sharp, and that's why I can even be around normal people.

Kara's face set in determination. "You know what we should do? We should all run those stairs again. That was tough, but fun."

Bella grimaced. "I was sore for days after that. I don't know if I want to inflict that kind of pain on my legs again for a while. What about you, Shay?"

She shrugged. "I agree with Kara. It was fun. I think we should. I've also been kind of thinking of taking up parkour. It looks useful. Uh, I mean it looks like it could be a good workout."

Janelle gave Shay a suspicious look. "Parkour? Isn't that all that running and jumping off buildings stuff?"

"There's some of that, but it's not about being a daredevil, really. It's about using the environment and momentum to your maximum advantage. It's great, because not only do you get a good workout, it teaches you to be very aware of your surroundings."

Her friend shrugged and picked up her wine glass. "Sounds like a lot of work. I think I'll stick with the stairs."

The other women nodded their agreement.

Shay shrugged. "Whatever works."

She'd need to find a parkour group. Annoyance lingered in the back of her mind over how the cat burglar had eluded her. While ego had played a role, the practical implications of parkour-enhanced mobility weren't lost on her. As her most recent trip to Paris had demonstrated, being a tomb raider often took her away from blasted deserts or arctic wastelands to urban population centers.

Shay frowned. Training in parkour would mean having

to deal with a whole new group of people and even more lies, but it'd be easier than when she'd first befriended this trio.

Lying had always been easy, and it'd served her well in her old career. Lying to people she planned to see again had been a new experience, though, and all her practice made the whole process smoother. Fucked up, perhaps, but she wouldn't ignore the truth.

"Something wrong, Shay?" Bella inquired. "You were making a face for a second."

The tomb raider shook her head. "Just was thinking about this asshole I ran into the other day. Real cocky bastard. I really wanted to punch him in his smug face."

Bella laughed. "I think you just described half of LA."

"Just need to work out some of that nervous energy." Kara put her fork down on her empty plate. "I think we might need some parkour or a bunch of stairs after dessert, but if we ran those stairs every couple of days, I bet we could eat whatever we wanted."

Shay smiled to herself. She might have deviated from her life plan, but she still had a life. It was a compartmentalized and complicated threading of multiple identities, obligations, and goals, but it was still a life.

I'm living now, not just existing.

16

The morning sun was still climbing into the sky, with more than a few of the taller buildings in the east eclipsing the glowing orb.

Shay stretched her arms above her head as she looked at the other people gathered atop the roof in the business district that morning. Everyone had a vaguely similar look: lithe, and wearing loose-fitting shirts and pants.

Her own tank and sweatpants matched everyone's else style, but she'd gone for dark colors, whereas everyone else was wearing something brighter. She had no idea if that said something about her or the group.

The Free-to-Move website didn't say anything about a dress code, but I didn't look that hard.

A tall, lanky man with bushy brown hair walked her way and extended his hand. "Don't think I've seen you around before. I'm Aaron."

Shay looked him up and down. He stood with a relaxed air. There wasn't a hint of tension around him, despite the fact he was about to go running and jumping through half of LA.

"I'm Shay. You in charge?"

He shrugged. "We don't really do hierarchy or ranks. We feel it goes against the spirit of parkour. Freedom, you know? That's the way I look at it. I want to have maximum freedom, in my life and my movement."

"I've been…toying with the idea of parkour, but I feel like if I really want to learn it, I'll need to be around people who are proficient, if only to observe people better than me. I don't know about all the freedom sh…stuff, though."

Aaron smiled. "Yeah, watching others can help at first, but you'll soon realize how natural this all is and start improving your moves without even thinking about it. Just got to practice, practice, practice."

Shay had already taken to that mantra. She'd set up some walls, stairs, and platforms inside Warehouse One so she could at least train in parkour without drawing attention to her secret building. Her movements were still inelegant and her thought processes too direct, but at least it was a start.

Seeking out a group of experienced practitioners was the next natural step. At a minimum, they'd know parkour routes that wouldn't have too many issues with trespassing or official disapproval.

Aaron waved and turned. "Just try and keep up. If not, no shame."

A pony-tailed Asian woman sauntered up to Shay. "It's good to get a new girl in the group. These guys aren't super-full of testosterone, but it's still nice to up the chick balance." She extended her hand. "Lana."

"Shay." The woman had a firm shake.

"We don't do judgment here, but we also don't hold your hand. So don't feel bad if you can't keep up."

Shay chuckled. "Okay, I'll keep that in mind."

Aaron raised his arm. "Okay, everyone, time to get going. As a reminder, we're having our post meal at the Great Sandwich Hut this week. Go to the forum and vote if you want to eat somewhere else next time. Other than that, see you soon." He spun and sprinted toward the edge of the building.

Lana winked at Shay and jogged after him. Shay took a deep breath and followed.

Let's see if any of that practice has paid off.

The traceurs and traceuses leapt from the building at an angle, bright smiles on their faces. Shay was the last person to make the jump. Everyone landed with a smooth roll, even Shay.

So far, so good. I can do this.

Aaron and Lana were the first two up and running again. Shay managed to get to her feet before some of the others, but everyone else was moving forward before her.

They approached another ledge, but this time the next roof was higher rather than lower. The athletes all leapt and caught the edge, pulling themselves up, and jumping to their feet.

The light morning traffic flowed on the roads below them, the walkers never looking up and spotting the half-dozen people leaping from building to building as if gravity were a mere inconvenience.

Lana took the lead, leaping off the side of the building

onto a metal staircase and flipping backward over the railing to a narrow alley. Aaron and the others followed.

Shay knew her limitations. She didn't go for the flip, instead pushing off the railing. The split second of consideration cost her a few yards as the group sprinted down the alley.

Her heart galloped in her chest and sweat beaded on her face, but she smiled.

She didn't mind that she was pulling up the rear. Her parkour experience was limited, and the morning wasn't about catching an arrogant asshole, but training and expanding her skills.

The cat burglar had escaped because she hadn't been prepared, and this group would help ensure that never happened again.

For now, keeping up was impressive enough.

At last, a real challenge—one that makes me better and doesn't just piss me off.

Aaron and Lana vaulted over a trash bin in perfect sync. The woman landed with a roll, then burst into the air grabbing a windowsill and swinging, her toned arms taut, over to the next window. Aaron and then everyone else followed. Shay didn't pay attention to where they were going, instead concentrating on following the men and women in front of her.

There was a ledge at the end of the windows. Lana leapt to it and pulled herself up, followed by Aaron.

The minutes flowed together, and Shay's focus centered on the people in front of her. She grinned, the pain in her legs and lungs as distant as if it were happening to someone else entirely.

Rooftops and stairs gave way to the street, then a park. Shay pulled ahead of a few members, but she couldn't close on Aaron and Lana.

Aaron rushed into an empty playground. He leapt into the air and grabbed the top bar of a swing set, only releasing when he had a perfect 45-degree angle. He sailed over a fence with ease. Lana repeated the move, then everyone else.

Shay fell into the rear again, but she executed the fence jump, missing the top by mere inches. She let out a laugh.

I could have hurt myself there, but I just don't give a damn.

The group pounded down a sidewalk, rushing past a frowning businessman chattering on his phone. Shay resisted the urge to comment.

Aaron led the swift procession into a path between two buildings. Not an alley, really, since it was barely large enough for a motorcycle to fit through. He launched himself from the top of a metal FedEx box toward the wall, then alternated pushing off from the walls on either side until he arrived at a balcony. He grabbed the balcony and launched himself into the street.

Several seconds passed until Shay's brain recognized the danger, but Aaron didn't plummet to his death. Instead, he caught the edge of another balcony and used his new handhold to swing to yet another.

These look like apartments. Would probably annoy someone if they noticed. So much for my theory that these guys would avoid routes that might attract attention. Still don't give a damn, though.

They dropped from balcony to balcony until they

reached the ground again, and broke into a sprint. Miles now separated the group from their starting point.

The group avoided vaulting anyone's cars. Shay could appreciate their desire to avoid property damage, since that was far more likely to attract police attention than being on someone's balcony for a second. The next minutes blurred together, her body and concentration pushed to the limit.

A vault, roll, and abrupt stop by Aaron in a parking lot caught her by surprise. She stumbled but didn't fall.

Shay bent over, taking several deep breaths. It'd been a long time since she'd been so challenged. Even the asshole cat burglar's little escape game hadn't pushed her as hard as Free-to-Move.

The others exchanged high-fives.

Lana walked over to Shay, sweat coating her face. "Not bad, newbie."

"Thanks." Shay just breathed for a moment. A deep intake of air helped, and she wiped her face. "That was damned hard."

"You impressed me. We get a lot of wannabes, and I like I said, we don't judge, but I feel bad because almost no one can complete an entire course the first time."

Shay shrugged. "I might not have done much parkour, but I exercise a lot, and I've got my own obstacle course I train on. At least the muscle strength carries over."

Aaron stepped over to the women. "Congrats. You'll have to run another course with us at our next meeting. We have to get you past the beginner course."

"Beginner course? Fuck me!" Shay laughed. "Not that I won't try."

Aaron and Lana both clapped her on the shoulder.

The ache in Shay's body didn't bother her. It was a badge of accomplishment and told her where she needed to direct her physical training. The obstacle course and the boxing gym were useful, but she still had holes in her training—and unlike James, she couldn't depend on an alien amulet or alien strength.

Plus, I still need to show up that asshole from the other night. Huh. Maybe they've heard of him.

Shay cleared her throat. "Hey, when I was looking some stuff up on local parkour groups, I saw some shit on a forum about a cat burglar who uses parkour. Do you think that's real, or is it just some sort of urban legend?"

Aaron and Lana's smiles vanished, and for the first time that morning they tensed.

Yeah, looks like they know him, all right.

Lana looked at Aaron.

He gave her a slow nod. "I'll catch up with you. I'm going to go get our table."

Shay spotted the yellow sign declaring they were at the Great Sandwich Hut.

"Don't worry about it." Aaron nodded toward Lana. "She'll answer your questions."

Shay blinked as the other members of Free-to-Move made their way into the restaurant.

She frowned. "What's the big deal? Why is everyone so spooked?"

"Marcus," Lana declared.

"Huh?"

"That's his name. The cat burglar. Marcus." She averted her eyes. "We knew him. He used to run with us."

"Shit. Seriously?"

"Yeah. Gifted. One of the best ever. He makes even a young David Belle look slow and clumsy when he's really trying."

Really trying? Was that fucker just toying with me the other night, then? Asshole.

Shay nodded. "What happened?"

"Nobody knows. Marcus was always an easy-going guy. A while back, he started talking about a string of robberies in unusual places, high apartments that had been broken into and buildings that had been entered from the roof. He was talking about how weird that was. Some people even said there might be magic involved."

"I remember reading about that."

"We thought he was just obsessed with it until at one point he admitted it was him. He talked about how rich we could become using our skills. He gave a big speech about how the people he robbed deserved it."

"Fuck. What happened? What did you do?"

Lana shrugged. "What *could* we do? We called the cops, but they could never find him. He's still in LA, but he's running with a very rough crowd. You shouldn't even *try* to go looking for him. He's dangerous."

Shay resisted a snort.

I doubt he's more dangerous to me. He might have gotten away, but if I'd wanted to kill him, I could have.

"Thanks for letting me know. I'll keep that in mind."

Lana managed a smile. "No problem." She nodded toward the restaurant. "Let's go get some breakfast."

Shay's phone buzzed, and she pulled it out. Peyton. "You go on ahead. This might be important."

"Sure thing." Lana waved and headed inside, a troubled look lingering on her face.

"What's up?" Shay answered.

"There's a job on the table."

"So? We can talk about it later this afternoon."

"No can do."

"Why?"

"It's a time-sensitive job that's in Russia and out of this world."

Shay rolled her eyes at the pride in the man's voice over his wordplay. "Fine. I'll be there as soon as possible."

Fuck. Guess I'll call an Uber to take me back to my car.

17

Shay snapped her head around at a foghorn blast from the bay. A small fishing vessel puttered along, but a blue speedboat rushed past them, missing them by feet.

What an asshole.

She narrowed her eyes, not liking being back in Russia and near water, even if she had no reason to believe that *vodyanoy* or *rusalka* were waiting to drag her into the bay. Vladivostok might not be LA, but it also wasn't some pissant village in the hinterlands.

That rusalka *bitch had delusions of grandeur, though. Who knows where she might end up?*

Shay shook her head. She needed to concentrate on the current job.

A few chatting dockworkers pointed toward the fishing boat and rattled off something in Russian. Even though they weren't talking to her, the lack of understanding annoyed her.

I can't depend on translation software. I keep coming back here, so maybe I should look into studying Russian.

Shay made her way down the road, sparing looks for the workers, trucks, cranes, and forklifts scattered up and down the docks.

If Peyton's information was correct, the old woman holding the artifact Shay was interested in ran a small bait shop in the area. After locating the artifact, the tomb raider could figure out how to best acquire it with minimum attention from the local authorities.

A few dockworkers eyed her as she passed them. She had elected to wear a brown wig and a simple dress to attract less attention, but she wasn't fading into the background enough.

Would jeans and a leather jacket have worked better?

Shay chuckled, still not sure about the job. Her thoughts drifted back to Peyton's briefing.

"What's the big rush?" Shay asked as she stepped into the office of Warehouse Two. "I didn't stop to take a shower because you were whining about me getting here, so this better damn well be as time-sensitive as you claimed."

"Sure is. The rush is that we've got a job, and it pays well. Not only does the client want a real quick turnaround, someone's already on the way to collect the artifact."

"Did the client hire them?"

"Nope. I stumbled onto them when I was doing some background research." He grinned. "You're going to love this."

Shay narrowed her eyes. "Who is it?"

"Guess."

She scrubbed her face with her hand. "Francois-fucking-Durand?"

Peyton clicked a few times on his computer and a fuzzy picture of Francois Durand appeared on the screen. He was an athletic middle-aged man with close-cropped blond hair. Attractive enough, but he lacked James' solid build or the handsome face of many of the local Hollywood stars.

"I was double-checking the client information when I got some alerts."

Shay frowned. "That means this is Project Nephilim shit, then? Alien stones?"

"Not exactly."

"Not exactly?"

Peyton nodded. "The short version is that a few decades back, a Russian man found a small piece of metal embedded in some coal he was using to light a fire. He took that metal to local scientists, and their examinations revealed it was a tooth-wheel made of pure aluminum."

Shay snorted. "Wow. That's spectacularly unimpressive. I can find aluminum in my kitchen drawer."

"The problem was, the wheel was embedded in the coal. As in, the coal had formed around it, and that coal was three hundred million years old. The wheel showed every indication of having been machined. It wasn't like humans were around to whip up tooth-wheels back then unless they were using time travel."

"Okay, I admit that's more impressive. So, best bet is alien litter?"

Peyton shrugged. "Maybe."

"Does it have any symbols on it?"

"Not that I could find reported, but I don't know the extent of the examination. The information on it is pretty light on the details."

Shay snorted. "Could be bullshit. Just because a lot of weird shit has turned out to be true doesn't mean it all is."

"True enough, but the client's willing to drop a million for its recovery."

"That's a pretty strong motivation."

Peyton laughed. "I thought you'd say that. Or you could not take the job and just grab it."

"Nah. I'll image the shit out of it before I turn it over, and you know what? The fact that Durand is looking for it is enough proof for me that it has something to do with alien shit, and I'm not gonna let that guy grab any alien artifacts first. Who's the client? The Professor? Correk?"

Peyton shook his head. "A Cypriot antiquities collector who now lives in Hawaii. The guy's very clean. He spent years running charities. Made most of his money in biotech research, but cashed out early to focus on his eccentric interest in proving that aliens inhabited the Earth millions of years ago. The only odd thing is that he's made it clear that somebody already owns the wheel."

"Why didn't he just buy it from them?"

"From what he said, he wants to keep his involvement really low-key. Claims that Men in Black showed up to threaten him a few days ago, which is one of the reasons he was pushing for this to happen quickly. He didn't mention Durand, though, so I don't think he knows about him."

Shay rolled her eyes. "Those guys were probably Project Nephilim assholes." She took a deep breath. "Did he specifically mention any restrictions on how I could recover the wheel?"

Peyton shook his head. "Nope, only that he needs it ASAP."

"And who has it now?"

"Marina Mikhailova. She runs a bait shop in Vladivostok. The weird thing is, it's hard to figure out how she got the artifact since the wheel disappeared from history after the original owner died. Even the client was a bit fuzzy on how he found out she had it." Peyton eyed Shay. "Ignoring all that, are you ready to steal from an old lady?"

Shay glared at the image of the French retrieval specialist on the screen. "If Durand and Project Nephilim are after it, it might be better for her if she didn't have that wheel when they showed up."

Peyton chuckled. "So you're saying you're doing her a favor by taking it from her?"

"I'm saying that the world's an imperfect place." Shay nodded toward her car. "Guess we should get to Warehouse Three and get my gear ready."

Shay continued marching down the dock in her search for the bait shop. Everything she'd told Peyton was true. She wasn't about to gun down some old woman for an artifact, but she wasn't leaving Russia without the wheel. It's not like some babushka needed the damned thing anyway.

Better not to ever mention to James that I'm robbing old ladies. I don't think he'd understand, even if I gave him the speech about the Men in Black.

She'd also have to explain what the hell Project Nephilim was, and how his alien amulet might even be connected to a greater secret. The OCD man could barely stand his house having a few stray particles of dust. There was no way he could handle being at the center of some massive history-changing revelation like that.

That's your problem, James. You want life to be simple. KISS and all that, but life's never simple, and the more you try to force it to be that way, the more it snaps back and makes things even crazier.

Shay sighed. For once in her life, one of her lies wasn't self-serving.

She shook her head and looked around. The damned shop was supposed to be close, according to the information Peyton had provided. She grabbed her phone to call him.

No bars.

Even if she ignored the cell tower she could see a few hundred yards away, her phone should have automatically switched to satellite mode when she lost the cell signal. There were several possible explanations for the glitch, but given the situation, one seemed most likely: someone was jamming the phone.

Pulling that off in the middle of a city took balls, since it'd draw the attention of authorities sooner rather than later.

Shay slowed her pace and surveyed her surroundings. The area was empty, the nearest dockworkers far behind her. It wasn't like farther up the docks there was a huge crowd, but the sudden absence of *anyone* was notable.

Three black SUVs with tinted windows had parked farther up, past rows of storage buildings, small shops, and the occasional maritime office.

Too shiny. Too fancy. The vehicles didn't fit the docks at all.

Shay jogged toward the vehicles and slowed when she caught sight of three large suited men standing near a small shop sandwiched between two shuttered stores with cracked windows. She couldn't understand any of the Cyrillic writing on the store's signage, which otherwise only decorated with a small picture of a silver fish.

One of the men frowned at her, and she turned around to walk the other way. She ducked around a corner so she could come up on the shop from behind.

A muffled scream came from the shop. Shay pulled her gun from her purse, regretting not being in her jacket and pants. She'd hoped to blend with the local fashions, but the dress wasn't the best for tactical movement.

She closed on the back door of the shop, gun raised. A woman shouted in Russian and someone spoke back, their voice calm and measured. Shay couldn't make out the second speaker through the door.

Three... Two... One...

The tomb raider knocked the door off its hinges with a solid kick.

Let's see Marcus pull that *shit off.*

Shay rushed into the back room, her gun at the ready. Stacked wooden crates lined the walls, and a shelf filled with cleaning supplies was in the center.

She ignored the room and ran to the next door and threw it open. She turned the corner and spotted an old woman, her face weathered by the decades and salty air.

An all-too-familiar athletic blond man with close-cropped hair loomed over the babushka. He had her backed up against a wall.

The three goons stood outside, their backs to the front windows, but Shay had no idea how long that would last.

"Francois Durand," Shay spat.

The man glanced at her with a smile. "Aletheia. We finally meet." His French accent was slight but still noticeable.

Shay narrowed her eyes. "You know who I am?"

"I knew you'd come sniffing around eventually. You've made such a name for herself. Curiosity compels you maybe, but you shouldn't stick your nose into this matter, tomb raider."

Shay lifted her gun. "Fuck you, Durand. I've got a job to do."

The babushka rattled off something in Russian and glared at the Frenchman. She looked like she wanted to tear him apart with her teeth.

"I've got a job to do as well." He nodded downward as if pointing to something.

Shay's jaw tightened. The man already had his gun out and had aimed it at the old woman.

What an asshole. This is gonna get bloody. Got to convince him to back the hell off.

She sneered. "Whatever. She's not my problem. I'm just here for the artifact, and I'm not leaving without it."

Durand gave Shay a sly smile. "Ah, I have heard about how ruthless you are. All those men you killed on Oak Island, for example. They say it was a massacre. How cold."

"You think I give a fuck about killing a few mercenaries?"

"No, I suppose you don't."

Shay smirked. "If you know all that, then you should know that I'm not to be fucked with."

Keeping his gun pointed at the old woman, Durand shrugged. "And you should know I have the backing of powerful people. You'd be wise not to attract too much of our attention."

"Project Nephilim? They're nothing but a bunch of idiots who can't figure shit out, which is why they have to overpay your ass to run around the world doing busywork, and why they have to hide in the shadows."

Durand's mouth twitched.

Oh, so you know a lot of shit, but you didn't realize I knew a lot of shit too, huh?

The bell above the front door jingled, and the three goons from before stepped in, guns out, frowning.

"They can't kill me before I kill you, Durand," Shay hissed.

"That's likely true, but don't you see? It doesn't have to be this way. I respect you, Aletheia, for accomplishing so much when you're new to the field. At first I thought you were an old veteran who'd changed her name, but now that I've seen you, I know that you're newer at this. Walk away. I've already beaten you to the woman."

"So what? You think she's gonna give up the artifact to a douchebag like you? She looks like she wants to tear off your balls right now."

The woman nodded. She must have understood more English than Shay suspected.

Durand chuckled. "I must say I'm disappointed that you haven't realized it yet." He pointed with his free hand to a plaque above the shop counter. Cyrillic writing adorned the bottom, but there was nothing else but a worn brass plaque.

"I don't get it, Durand. You like featureless decorations?"

With a sly grin, the retrieval specialist reached into his pocket and pulled out a shiny tooth-wheel. "You see? I never needed to get the location from her."

Shay narrowed her eyes, her heart rate kicking up. "What the fuck? Then why are you still there? Why are you even bothering to threaten the old woman? Do you get off on it?"

"No, no. I don't tend to like unnecessary bloodshed, but sometimes it's necessary. In this case, though I couldn't resist the chance to meet you."

The babushka muttered something under her breath and gave Durand a baleful glare.

Shay gritted her teeth. "Let me make this very fucking clear, Durand. I don't care how badass you think you are or how much some government douchebags are paying you to accept their leash. I've killed a lot of people a lot of ways in a lot of places, and I don't see any reason why I shouldn't paint the walls of this shop fucking red with the blood of you and your asshole friends."

Durand sighed. "You know the other reason I set up this little farce?"

"You have a small penis and you're compensating?"

He chuckled. "Reputation's a curious thing. Not solid, not real. Ephemeral. When you're evaluating someone, the best thing to do is to observe them in action."

He pointed the gun straight at the old woman's stomach. She frowned but didn't say anything.

Shay's attention flicked between Durand and the three goons. A single shot would start a storm of lead, but if she timed it right, she could win.

"Do you have a point, Durand, or are you just trying to bore me into leaving?"

"My point is, I've learned something through observing you. For example, you arrived here only minutes after me, which means you're fast, resourceful, and intelligent.

"You were also careful enough to come in the back rather than just gun down my friends over there and kick open the door. That was enough to confirm your reputation as a tomb raider of some skill. My other concern is that you've survived encounters with dangerous foes. At least twice you've run into Snegurka and survived."

"She's a real bitch, you know."

The babushka glanced between Shay and Durand with a confused look on her face.

Durand held up a finger. "It's not surprising that you'd live up to your tomb-raiding reputation, but there's something else that's hard to know without seeing it in person. Something I now just confirmed."

"And what's that?"

"How truly ruthless you are. For all I knew, you were only defending yourself when you killed in the past. There's a certain practicality to that, but it's not the same thing as a killer instinct."

Shay gave him a feral grin. "You don't want to test my killer instinct, Durand."

"But I already have. Don't you see?"

"What the fuck are you talking about?"

"If you were truly the killer you're trying to convince

me you are, you would have shot this woman and me the minute you stepped in."

"Shit."

Durand barked out a laugh.

Fuck it.

Shay leapt toward the counter and put a bullet into Durand's chest. Three quick shots followed before the goons even comprehended a gunfight had started and they collapsed to the ground, their blood pooling together.

The tomb raider hit the floor and rolled onto her back, ready to fire at anyone coming around the corner. The bell above the front door jingled, and she jumped to her feet, her gun still out. Durand sprinted away from the shop.

What the hell?

As he turned, the bulletproof vest under his torn shirt peeked out.

"Damn it. Of course, he had to be fucking careful."

Shay hopped the counter and looked at the old woman. She was shaking her fist at the front door.

"You okay?" Shay inquired.

"You go," the woman snapped in heavily accented English. "You go shoot last thief."

Shay grinned. "Sounds like a good plan to me." She rushed to the front door. The tomb raider ran after the retrieval specialist, not bothering to squeeze off pistol shots because of the distance.

Durand reached into his jacket.

Going for a gun?

He tossed something her way. Something small and round. A grenade.

"Shit." Shay jumped behind a cement pylon and closed her eyes.

The grenade didn't explode. A hiss sounded, and a thick cloud of dark gray smoke choked her.

Shay coughed and ran through the smoke. The air in front of her cleared, and her eyes widened at Durand in the distance leaping from a wooden pier into a blue speedboat —the same speedboat she'd seen almost hit the fishing boat earlier.

Of course, it was you, asshole.

She squeezed off several rounds, but none came close to striking the man or the boat. The engine roared to life and the speedboat shot away from the dock.

"Great. Just great." Shay dropped her gun back into her purse and pulled her phone out. Still no signal.

Francois Durand had escaped with the artifact, and she couldn't even contact Peyton to get a drone on him.

Shay sighed.

I hope you appreciate it, old lady. I just traded a million dollars for your life.

"This isn't over, Durand. I'm gonna find you, you prick."

18

Shay paced in front of the Warehouse Two office, her arms crossed. "That French asshole is really getting on my nerves."

Peyton turned a corner, a small bowl of water in hand, and walked over to set it down near the door to the office. Osiris meowed from underneath a nearby table and padded over to the bowl, his eager tongue flicking to lap up water.

"It's not a big deal, if you think about it," Peyton suggested.

Shay stopped and spun toward him, pinning him with a glare. "How the fuck isn't it a big deal? He got the artifact, and not only do I *not* get a million dollars, but this is gonna ding my rep."

Peyton shrugged. "I meant to tell you earlier, but based on the last message he sent, the client doesn't seem to care. Don't think he's going to say anything to hurt your reputation."

"He doesn't *care?*" Shay narrowed her eyes. "What's going on?"

If the client had set her up, she was going to go have a loud and painful one-way conversation with him.

"I've got a pretty good feel for how this guy thinks by now, so I decided to really play up that guys in dark suits—you know, Men in Black—had shown up, and how you were forced to save the little old lady from the evil international government conspiracy." Peyton laughed. "He ate that up, and you know, it's basically true."

Shay groaned and slumped against a wall. "I didn't... save her. I just didn't shoot her when I had a chance."

I could have gotten the wheel if I had just opened fire immediately. Would it have been worth it for a million dollars?

She'd killed a lot of people in her life, and while she couldn't claim that every one of them had it coming, gunning down some unarmed old woman would have strayed into territory she hadn't dared enter.

That didn't mean they needed to discuss the subject. Shay couldn't dismiss the moderating effects of James, Alison, and all her new friends on her personality, but she refused to be anyone's open book. She was sleeping with James and she still kept things from *him*, let alone her assistant.

Peyton shrugged. "I've always been a lover, not a fighter. Not saying I have a problem with you taking down some of the assholes you have, but it's not so bad that you're a little less vio—" He blinked under her enraged glare. "Uh, let's stop talking about that."

"I agree. We should stop talking about that."

He swallowed and took a deep breath. "Anyway, the

client doesn't blame us. He blames the government conspiracy, and from what he told me, he thinks that the fact that even *Aletheia* couldn't recover the artifact because of the government is proof that everything he believes in is real. He almost seemed giddy about it in his messages. He's not giving up, and has mentioned hiring you for future jobs once he has a line on other alien artifacts."

"That doesn't change anything about the last job." Shay shook her head. "That French fucker stole my artifact and messed with me on a job. It's one thing to lose to Yulia. She's at least a witch, but that guy doesn't have any magic." She pointed at the computer in the office. "Find Durand. Drop everything else for now. I don't want any other jobs until I can find him again. The important thing is Francois Durand, and the wheel he stole from me. Asshole got lucky by showing up a few minutes earlier. He's not better than me."

"You planning to kill him?"

Shay shrugged. "Maybe, but mostly it's time he realized he's not free to do whatever the hell he wants. It might be good *not* to kill him."

"Huh? Why?"

"Because where he goes there will be alien artifacts, and next time, I want to be the one holding the artifact and mocking *him*."

Shay leapt from the roof of the office building and landed with a smooth roll on the next building. She ran close to the edge to keep Durand's black SUV in sight. The dense DC traffic was slowing him down, which helped.

Peyton's and Shay's research had managed to turn up a plane itinerary placing Durand in Washington DC, and a quick trip across the country was far more practical than waiting for the next time the asshole showed up halfway across the world. That didn't mean shadowing the French retrieval specialist was easy.

Now that Shay was onto the man, she had only her skills to draw on. She had no open line to Peyton and no drones. Electronics could fail or be traced, and a paranoid asshole like Durand would be looking for something like that anyway. She doubted he'd bother to check the roofs of nearby buildings to see if someone was using parkour to trail him, though. Until a few days ago, she would have never thought of the idea herself.

Thanks, Marcus. Because you pissed me off, I've been learning a new useful skill. Next time I see you, I'll thank you after I punch you in the nose.

After a few more blocks of slow-moving traffic, the SUV pulled into a parking lot. Shay ducked and watched from the edge of her current roof.

Durand emerged, along with two other suited men. He gestured toward a tall office building across the street, but Shay was too far to hear away what he was saying.

Should get some sort of portable laser mic if I'm gonna be stalking guys through DC.

The men nodded and headed toward the crosswalk. Durand strode the opposite way, his hands in his pockets.

What are you up to, asshole? Got a meeting you don't even want any goons to overhear?

Now that her quarry was out of his vehicle, shadowing him from above was trivial. Shay continued jumping from rooftop to rooftop, with the help of the occasional ledge or balcony. Durand continued walking at a swift but not extreme pace, as if he had plenty of time to arrive at his eventual destination.

Just taking a stroll? Looking for your favorite bakery?

Durand glanced around every once in a while, but never up. Good instincts, just not good imagination. Shay grinned.

Hitting the ground at this point would only increase the chance he'd spot me. I'll just follow him to wherever he's going and figure out how to handle him from there.

The blond man stopped right in front of an alley and spent even longer than usual looking around. Once finished, he ducked into it, disappearing from view.

"Damn it."

Shay sprinted forward to get a better viewing angle on the alley from the roof. Durand was nowhere in sight, but he hadn't time to walk all the way down the alley either. Several doors faced the alley, but none were open.

Doubt you teleported, you slippery bastard. Which door? Guess I have to get closer.

Shay jumped from the roof edge onto a fire escape, grabbed the handrail and flipped down to a nearby balcony, then to a closed trash bin. A quick jog across the street brought her to the mouth of the alley after a few loud horn blasts from angry motorists.

She entertained herself with the thought that she'd just pissed off some douchebag Congressman.

The back doors to several buildings—restaurants, by

the looks of them—opened into the alley. Boxes, trash bags, and two commercial-sized green garbage bins were in the alley, but there was no sign of Durand.

He went in one of these buildings, but which one?

Shay took a few careful steps forward and searched for a stray footprint or handprint that might mark the man's trail.

"Impressive, Aletheia," commented an annoyingly familiar French voice from behind her.

The tomb raider spun and yanked out her gun.

Durand already had his gun out and pointed at her, an amused smirk on his face.

Shay narrowed her eyes. "Why didn't you shoot me when you had the chance?"

"It's as I told you before—I'm impressed with you. Very few people can follow me for any length of time without me being aware of it. Not only that, the fact you could even find me to follow me is impressive. Even though I don't hide behind an alias like you, it's not as if I announce my movements to the world." He gave her a cheerful grin and shrugged. "I'm guessing, though, that you aren't here to kill me."

"That's undecided as of yet, asshole."

"So feisty. If this is about the wheel, you're too late. It's already been passed along to my clients. Even if you tortured me for days, you wouldn't recover it."

"Your clients at Project Nephilim?"

The corner of Durand's mouth turned up. "You've made a lot of assumptions, but that doesn't mean I need to verify them. You know far less than you think you do." He gestured with his gun toward her. "Put your weapon away and I'll stow mine, or we could try to kill each other now. It seems a pointless waste of talented lives, but it's a cruel world we inhabit."

He's probably wearing a vest, so I'd have to tag him in the head, but I'm not wearing a vest because of mobility, so he gets my head and whole center of mass for lethal target practice.

Shay slowly lowered her gun. Durand mirrored her movement, and both holstered their weapons under their jackets.

The Frenchman let out a contented sigh. "It's so easy to accidentally shoot someone. That feels much better, don't you think?"

"We'll have to agree to disagree on that."

"Don't be so annoyed, Aletheia. You're much better at this than I was when I started, but you're still a..." He frowned. "What's a good word? Trainee, perhaps? Ah, I know." He snapped. "Still a *rookie*."

"I'm not a fucking rookie. My record speaks for itself."

Durand shrugged. "From my perspective you are. I've been doing this a lot longer than you have. I long ago even abandoned the silly pretension of calling myself a 'tomb raider' or 'field archaeologist.'"

Shay snorted. "Oh, 'retrieval specialist' is so much better?"

"There's a certain clarity to it, but it also reflects the larger scope of what I do. I *retrieve* things, not just from musty old ruins or strange out-of-the-way places, but sometimes, as you saw, from people who no longer deserve to have them."

"How useful you are."

Durand shrugged and scratched his cheek. "You're on

your way to becoming more than a mere tomb raider. That's something to look forward to." He clucked his tongue. "So many interesting adventures! Pulling those artifacts off the Mahogany Ship for instance, and whatever you were doing in Paris. I don't know what you were after, but there certainly was a lot of strange things reported, even though using an EMP like that in a crowded area was a sloppy move."

Shay didn't care if that hadn't been her fault. The retrieval specialist didn't need to know anything about her. Just because they weren't shooting each other in that alley didn't mean things wouldn't end in blood eventually.

"You think I'm gonna tell you anything?" Shay snapped.

"No, I don't, but as I've just proven, I know more about you than you know about me. I'm going to give you a little friendly advice, Aletheia. You need to stop poking your nose into my work. You've already lost the wheel, so you have no reason to follow up on any of this just because you think you know a few things."

"Like the fact you snatched a three hundred-million-year-old out-of-place artifact from an old lady?"

"It's just a hunk of metal. In many ways, it's worthless."

Shay snorted. "It was worth a million dollars to me, and if it's so worthless, why did your employers care enough to have you go get it?"

He waved a hand dismissively. "People can misinterpret things. Sometimes it's best to just help them not do that. See, even you have made a few leaps of logic, you've taken a few things out of context and read a few rumors online and convinced yourself of something that's not true."

"You don't know what I believe or know."

Durand chuckled.

Shay stared at him, not saying anything for several seconds. For all his smugness and skills, he wasn't infallible. From what he'd said, he obviously believed she only knew about him through the Project Nephilim records, and he hadn't alluded to the alien stone she'd recovered from Mexico.

He doesn't know I have it. He also doesn't know about the one I grabbed for the Professor, or about Correk.

She was finally ahead of Durand.

Shay allowed herself a smirk. "Guess we'll just see what happens. Exciting shit."

Durand backed up slowly toward the street. At least he was smart enough not to turn his back on her.

"Don't assume that next time I won't deal with you more violently," he warned.

"Don't make promises you can't keep, asshole."

With a final wave, Durand stepped out of the alley and headed in the direction of the parking lot.

Shay took a few steps before stopping. Following him after he'd already surprised her was pointless. She gritted her teeth and tightened her hands into fists.

Think you're better than me, Durand? I respect you for spotting me, but I'm gonna end up the best tomb raider, and I'm not gonna let you scare me off this alien shit.

S hay crossed her legs and stared at James' tv. No matter how many times he insisted they watch some cooking show focusing on barbeque, she could never get into it. It wasn't a matter of food preferences. As much as she loved pizza, the idea of watching a show about it didn't appeal. Tasting food was always better than looking at it.

"What's this again?" she inquired.

James leaned forward, his face scrunched in concentration. "The start of the new season of *Barbeque Wars: The Next Generation*. A lot of fair-weather barbeque fans won't be watching, though." He shook his head, disappointment on his face. "Idiots."

"Why's that? Did the producers get accused of lewd acts with a llama or something?"

"Nope. It's all human competitors this season. Not saying Nadina doesn't bring something special to the barbeque world, but people need to remember all the quality human pit masters."

Shay snickered. "Yeah, fuck those Oricerans. Earth! Earth! Earth! USA! USA! USA!"

Watching barbeque shows might not be fun, but teasing her man about them was.

James grunted. "It's not about that. I don't care as long as people make good barbeque, but it's not supposed to be solely about novelty." He shrugged. "You know what? We should head to Vegas soon and go to Jessie Rae's."

"James, I don't hate barbeque, but I don't love it so much that I want to marry it, unlike you. I'm not going all the way to Vegas just for some barbeque."

"While we're there we can do some other shit, too."

Shay thought that over for a few seconds and nodded. Getting a little sweaty in some nice silk sheets in a fancy resort might be fun, at least when she had the time for it.

"I'm in the middle of some job shit right now, but maybe in a few weeks."

"Hell, when summer vacation starts, we should go grab Alison and take her there. She told me that going to that Broadway show was really fun. She could really see the energy of the crowd and the performers, and she wants to see more shows like that."

"Yeah, Alison... I guess that can work."

Shay stopped herself from sighing. So much for a hot and sweaty weekend of passion.

It wasn't like she could complain about James wanting to spend more time with the girl he was in the process of adopting, and, for that matter, a girl she liked. While Shay wasn't ready to think of her as a daughter like James, she couldn't dismiss that the girl had become important to her.

A quiet chuckle escaped her mouth.

This is the problem with all new parents: their cockblock kids.

James looked at Shay, confused. "What's so funny?"

"Oh, nothing. Uh, was just thinking of some weird-ass outfit Peyton was wearing the other day."

"He really does like his freaky outfits."

She shrugged. "He considers them fashion-forward."

James grunted. "Whatever the fuck *that* means."

Shay laughed.

Good. I should let this shit distract me. The last thing I need to do is let James figure out that I was running around DC going after another tomb raider who is knee-deep in alien shit.

James picked up the remote and turned the tv off. Shay didn't bother to harass him about using voice recognition. Even *he* got annoyed with a joke run into the ground.

"Your show wasn't over," Shay pointed out. "You don't have to stop it because of me. I'll live. Maybe I'll learn something about barbeque."

"I can watch it later. I like re-watching them anyway."

"Even though you have a photographic memory?"

"A memory isn't like living through something." James shook his head. "We should talk. All the websites say so."

Shay rolled her eyes. "Do they, now?"

James nodded. "Yeah. So, how you holding up?"

"Huh? What are you talking about? I'm fine."

"Just saying, you said all that shit about the old Shay Carson being dead after we took out the cartel. I may not be good with this sharing feelings crap, but all this alien shit has taught me a thing or two about having to leave your old life behind."

Shay held up a hand. "Seriously, James, I'm fine. I still

have to be careful, but I don't feel like I need to look over my shoulder as much with the cartel wiped out."

"You sure?"

"Yeah. Why you asking?"

James frowned and looked away. "I don't know. I'm still new at this relationship shit, but sometimes I feel like you're hiding something from me."

Damn it, James. Half the time you're as observant as a brick, but now *you have to start paying attention?*

Shay placed a hand on his cheek. "Look, I've spent my entire life never trusting anyone but myself. This shit's gonna take time. It's not you, it's me."

He grimaced. "Shit, the websites talked about that, too."

She laughed. "Okay, bad word choice, but you know what I mean. Don't let it get to you. If anything important comes up, I'll let you know."

Trust me, James. I'm hiding this for your own good. You aren't ready for the weight of knowing about all this government alien program shit.

James grunted. "If you need some ass-kicking help on a raid, you know you can ask me."

"Yeah, yeah, but if I get too used to dragging your ass along I'm gonna get sloppy."

"Just saying."

Shay patted James on the shoulder. "Not to mention, a lot of times tomb raids require finesse. I love you, but you have the finesse of rabid junkyard dog."

"Ass-kicking doesn't require finesse."

"Tomb raids aren't usually about ass-kicking. It's not always about just killing the first warlock you run into. Besides, you know what they say."

James frowned. "What?"

"'Absence makes the heart grow fonder.'"

———

Shay leaned over and stared at Peyton's screen. Dozens of file names filled it, but they all looked like gibberish to her.

"What am I looking at?"

"Other files I found on government servers," Peyton explained.

Osiris lay on the table right in front of the mouse. He watched his owner move it back and forth as if plotting to attack the peripheral.

"And what's so special about these government files? Lists of politicians' favorite porn or something?"

Peyton chuckled. "I think seeing that would scar me. No, it turns out there's more to Project Nephilim than what I originally found. It also turns out the only reason I could even get those files is that they weren't as protected as they could have been."

"Seriously?"

"I think they're not as important as other stuff. Lower priority."

Shay blinked. "Wait, a secret government alien research program is *not* as important as something else?"

"Yep. There's another project, in addition to Houdini and Nephilim. Something else they seem to be dumping even more money into. Project Ragnarok."

"*Ragnarok*? Is Durand attached to that project as well?"

Peyton nodded. "I'm not a hundred percent sure, but I did find a few records that indirectly link him to Project

Ragnarok. I'm also guessing the project name isn't all that random." At Shay's raised eyebrow, he held up a hand. "Not saying they are planning the death of the Norse gods or something, but what if they know more about this alien stuff than we think? What if the Nephilim stuff was just some low-end work they shoved off for deniability? Or maybe they've figured out more since those Nephilim reports were submitted."

"What exactly are you getting at?"

"We, Earth humans, have regular contact with people from another world now, Oriceran. It's not like people's minds would be that blown if the government admitted there had been contact with another world besides Oriceran."

Osiris meowed and leapt off the table, apparently bored with the human chatter and fake plastic mice.

Shay glanced at the cat and back at Peyton. "The fact that they are being so damned secretive means they're worried about people panicking—the same people who already live in a world with necromancers and *rusalkas*. I know what I think that means."

Peyton nodded slowly. "I know what I think, too. What are *you* thinking?"

"I'm thinking that they're worried about a *War of the Worlds* situation, and also worried that all our technology and magic might not be enough. The question is, do they even have any evidence to be worried over, or are they just being paranoid?"

Peyton clicked around on his desktop and brought up a fuzzy picture of the aluminum tooth-wheel. "If aliens showed up that long ago with this level of technology, even if they were the slowest bastards in the galaxy they'd be way farther ahead of us. We'd be like ants trying to win against humans."

"But we don't just have tech now, we have magic."

Peyton shrugged. "What good is even the most powerful wand going to do if an alien mothership shows up and cracks the planet in half with a star-powered death ray?"

Shay stared at the image of the wheel, thinking through the possibilities. The memory of an earlier conversation in Russia with the rusalka floated back, unbidden.

There's something I sense in you...a destiny, perhaps. Something great or something horrible, but still grandiose. I want to see where that goes, and I don't think it ends with you being drowned in our local river.

The tomb raider chuckled. She'd believed Irina the *rusalka* had delusions of grandeur, but now she was letting them infect her own mind.

The truth of Project Ragnarok might be far more banal than she suspected, but it wouldn't hurt to keep looking into it. Even if it didn't even involve any dangerous alien invaders, the hidden knowledge and truth it represented called to Shay.

History should *be about the truth, but we were wrong for so many years. Not only that, people made sure we were wrong by hiding the truth. Fuck the government. This time they don't get to hide the truth, not from me.*

Shay looked at Peyton. "Keep poking around, but be careful. I have a feeling that if we end up poking too hard, a group of Special Forces guys in ski masks will bust through the door and gun our asses down."

Peyton swallowed. "Maybe…maybe it's best if we leave well enough alone? We're both trying to hide, after all. We don't have to do this. I know it's cool, but I kind of like continuing to breathe."

"Fuck that. James was right when he goaded me into taking down the cartel. Sometimes you shouldn't run. Sometimes you should charge in like a crazed rhino."

"I don't know if he's a bad influence on you or a good one." Peyton let out a nervous laugh. "Brownstone's a badass, but even if he helps you, it's not like you can take down the entire military by yourself."

"I'm not giving up on this." Shay stared Peyton down. "I'm also not gonna pull my gun and order you to poke around government systems. I'm just gonna tell you to grow a pair, but be careful when you do whatever it is you do. We've stumbled onto some major shit, and if we run away now, we might as well shoot ourselves, because we've already given up on living a life that means shit."

Peyton sighed. "Guess getting shot in the head by some Man in Black trying to protect a secret is almost as good as dying in bed after a long and healthy life."

Shay grinned. "Hey, as long I don't die in my kitchen, I don't care."

2 0

Shay pulled her Spider through the open loading bay door into Warehouse Three. She waited until the metal door slid closed, killed the engine, and stepped out of the car.

This better not be bullshit.

Peyton stood behind a long table, holding up and inspecting a small drone. He had a satisfied look on his face. He set the machine back down and picked up a headlamp. There were several pistols and magazines next to a tactical harness.

The tomb raider marched over to the table and crossed her arms, waiting in silence for the man to speak. He hadn't looked up since she'd entered the building.

"Wonder if I could add another sensor," Peyton mumbled. "Wish there was some easy way to detect magic."

Shay cleared her throat.

Peyton looked up. "Oh, hi. Didn't hear you come in."

"You didn't hear the massive metal door opening?"

"No, I didn't. Sorry."

Shay sighed. "You sent me a text and said it was important that I come here ASAP." She shrugged. "So I'm here. Now tell me *why* I'm here." She pointed to the table. "You're obviously getting my gear ready for a job, but you didn't tell me about anything."

"Oh, yeah, sorry for being so cryptic, I was working on something at the same time, so I was distracted when I sent the message. The short version is, yeah, I've got a new job lined up. I figured you needed a little something to soothe your ego and wallet after the whole debacle in Russia and Durand getting the better of you in DC."

Shay slammed a hand on the table, shaking the guns and electronics on top. "What the fuck?"

Peyton held up his hands. "A poor choice of words. Please don't harm the tech guy. If you do, you're honor-bound to take care of my cat."

Shay took a deep breath and slowly let it out. "Ignoring all that bullshit, I thought I told you I wanted to concentrate on Durand for a while. And, yeah, because of DC and Russia. Just because he got the drop on me in DC doesn't mean shit. I'm not through with him yet."

"Sure, sure, but because I'm so awesome, I figured out how to make money and still point you at Durand. Or point him at you. However you want to look at it."

Shay stepped away from the table and nodded slowly. "Okay, now I'm listening. Note that I'm the kinder, gentler Shay. I didn't even pull my gun."

Peyton smiled, but it looked forced. "I found a collector of rare art who is interested in Pre-Colombian-contact art.

He's interested in you recovering a solid gold Inca figurine for him, and he's willing to pay a million dollars."

"I'm liking the sound of this. Go on."

He pulled his phone out of his pocket and swiped until he located a picture of what looked like a stylized golden jet fighter. "This was created six hundred years ago, and, well, you can see how modern it looks."

Shay tilted her head back and forth to examine the picture from different angles. "Could be a coincidence. Maybe it's some Inca's funky version of a bird. I'd hate to see some alien grab a Cubist painting and think that's how things actually look on Earth."

"Sure, but a lot of people think it's not a coincidence. They used to say it proved alien contact, and some people even claimed they did the calculations involving a larger scale model of the design, and it was aerodynamic and would fly with appropriate thrust."

Shay nodded. "Okay. Interesting."

Peyton put his phone down. "Once everyone found out about Oriceran, they just assumed the ancient airplane was related to them."

"And how do we know it's not? Not saying I won't go after it for a million, but Durand might not be interested in this thing at all."

"People assumed, but they didn't check."

Shay arched a brow. "And you did?"

Peyton nodded. "I haven't found anything from an Oriceran source or related sources that mention them using anything that looks like this, and when you think it about it, it doesn't even make sense. A planet of magic users isn't going to run over to Earth and teach them about technological jet fighters."

"You make a good case."

Shay had long since passed the point of reflexive skepticism when it came to anything related to ancient aliens. Even ignoring everything she'd learned about Oriceran and aliens between James and the government searches, her previous tomb raids had involved her recovering things like activation artifacts for ancient Indian floating palaces. There was nothing too outlandish to dismiss out of hand anymore.

Those truths didn't mean every artifact hunt would lead her to new history, but if she had to bet, she'd bet on weird aliens or Oricerans more often than misinterpreted ancient art. Still, a few details remained unclear about the current job.

She pointed at the phone. "You have a modern picture of the thing, which means someone already has this. I think it's better if I try to avoid jobs that involve me having to fuck with people who already own something unless I have a damned good reason beyond money. I'm a tomb raider, not a cat burglar."

The morality of that type of artifact retrieval was still an open debate in her mind, but, at the minimum, she liked James' policy of only taking things from people who tried to kill him first. Fair and simple.

That policy also had the advantage of reducing the number of people, particularly law enforcement, who might come after her. Her recent if indirect brush with the FBI and LAPD AET served as a reminder of the dangers of enemies who didn't have to hide in the shadows.

Peyton looked to the side and nodded. "Oh, yeah. My fault for not being clearer. The client already has this one in his collection, but he's got a line on another one. Different design. Longer wings, and different shape. He's dubbed it 'the Bomber.' The client also got his hands on an old map from some nineteenth-century English explorers who were checking out rumors of Inca artifacts in the mountains of Ecuador."

"Ecuador, huh?"

Hitting a place where she could at least speak the language was always welcome, though she lacked any real contacts in the country. Given the way Peyton was acting, she doubted it'd be a problem.

"The map had a lot of holes," Peyton continued, "but there was enough information on the image they sent me to point me the right way. I've already done some analysis based on aerial surveys and satellite data, and I've found a suspicious site just begging to be checked out. It's sitting there singing, 'Come and get me, Shay.'"

She frowned. "Mighty convenient that no one has checked out the site before and found the figurine, don't you think?"

Peyton shook a finger. "But that's the thing. Even with the map, I had to do a lot of algorithmic imagery analysis to find the possible site. If you didn't already know exactly where to look, there would be no way to find it. No one's just going to stumble onto it."

"So we've got the location… Wait, if there's a map, and explorers already visited there, why didn't they already recover the Bomber?"

"Lots of rumors about guardians, and a note on the map

that when translated talks about scaly demons who eat men."

Shay chuckled. "At least they aren't frog-men. Any notes or rumors about these scaly demons being immune to guns?"

"Not that I've read."

"What about Durand? Find anything about him moving on the object?"

Peyton sighed and shrugged. "I've been trying to track him, but it's gotten a lot harder since he knows about you chasing him, so I have no idea. But the client only came into possession of this map within the last week. It's not like even if Durand heard about the artifact that he's had tons of time to get down there and find it, and that's assuming he actually has access to the map and the resources to figure it out."

"The asshole has the United States government behind him. I'm guessing there are more than a few imagery analysts working for Project Nephilim and Project Ragnarok. If we have an advantage, it's not gonna be in our ability to decode shit. We just got lucky with the symbols and the phrase because we had more samples than they did."

Peyton stuck out his lip and looked down. She'd poked his male ego, but she didn't give a damn. If Shay could acknowledge that Marcus was better at parkour and that Durand had at least a few skills that were better than hers, Peyton could deal with the fact he wasn't the only person in the country with decent research and computer skills.

Shay pointed to a shelf on the other side of the room. "Pack some jammers. Can never be too sure."

"You're going to take the job, then? I think you should, but I can't guarantee Durand will show up."

"It's an easy million if he doesn't, and if he does, it'll be a nice bonus."

"I already booked you a flight. Supersonic down to Quito. Leaves tonight."

"You were that certain I'd take the job?"

Peyton shook his head. "I was certain you'd want to take any chance to screw with Durand, even if it was a small one."

"You're right." Shay grinned. "Look out, Durand, this time I'm getting there first."

21

S hay slipped on her backpack, slammed the door of her rented Wrangler, and groaned. A mountain loomed over her, its peak disappearing into the thick clouds. Boulders and smaller rocks littered the ground in uneven piles. The way her Wrangler had bounced on the way up the mountain, she was surprised there weren't even more.

Looking at satellite photos hadn't prepared her for the extreme angle of the mountain.

Better than swimming to the bottom of some freezing lake.

This wouldn't be a leisurely hike, but a climb with full gear to a cave that might be hundreds of feet up. She needed to verify the cave's location before she bothered climbing anywhere.

Shay pulled out her phone but had no signal. Given that she was in the middle of a bunch of mountains, she wasn't suspicious or surprised. Cell towers had limited range. Satellites were impressive feats of engineering, but they still needed line of sight to work.

She brought up an app to scan the local frequency ranges. No indication of any artificial jamming. Nature was her only enemy at the moment, not a government stooge. That gave her some time, at least, even if she didn't relish the climb.

The physical challenge was one thing, but not all physical challenges were interesting. Obstacle courses and parkour offered variety that climbing a nearly-sheer cliff couldn't provide.

"Guess it can't all be fun and shooting," Shay muttered.

Her trip to the back of the Wrangler netted her a drone and her AR goggles.

A few minutes later, the drone hummed to life, the feed connected to her goggles. She piloted the drone, her stomach knotting as her brain adjusted to her eyes seeing the ground shrink even though her body didn't move. While she didn't always use the direct feed because of the feeling it gave her, it offered her a better inherent sense of distances and proportions.

Two hundred and fifty feet up, Shay found the cave. Too round, too perfect. Even if she hadn't been looking for a figurine allegedly inspired by aliens—if not outright made by them—she would have suspected the cave wasn't a natural formation.

Shay cycled from the visual band to IR. The display remained blue and black, with no current or residual heat signatures. Durand hadn't gotten here ahead of her this time.

Doesn't look like any scaly demons are hiding in there either. Those Brits shouldn't have let themselves be scared off so easily.

The drone maneuvered deeper into the cave, and Shay

switched back to the normal camera mode. She activated the main light on the drone, keeping it a foot under the low, smooth roof of the cave. Loose pebbles and stones lay on the floor, but there were no footprints. Ten feet inside, dramatic proof of something unusual appeared in the form of a solid-gold door.

The door gleamed under the drone's light, and there was a small flat panel where a handle might usually be.

"Huh. Guess there's no getting around just going up there, but at least I know there's something there."

Shay flew the drone back down and landed it next to the Wrangler. It was time for the annoying part of the job.

After grabbing a helmet with a headlamp from the SUV, she fished her rope and climbing supplies out of her backpack. She needed to find someone to supply her with a levitation ring for the next time she found herself in this sort of situation.

Stupid gnome. I'd ask you, but you're barely at your shop these days. Your cousin has probably moved to Mars by now because he figured out that Peyton was sniffing around.

"How the hell did the explorers even find this place? Use some magic they didn't admit to on their map? At least that means Monsieur Artiste Spécialiste de la Récupération won't be able to reach it."

The tomb raider smiled. There were no other vehicles in the area, and no other lines or any evidence that anyone had been to this part of the mountain in years. Her drone survey had proved no one else was around, human or monster.

Ha. You don't even know about this artifact, do you, Durand? Talking all that shit about me being a rookie, but I'm about to grab an alien artifact, or at least proof of aliens, and your precious Nephilim and Ragnarok assholes don't have a clue.

The smile left her face, and she sighed. She still had to climb the damned mountain.

"Good thing the stupid figurine is small," Shay muttered to herself. "And I wonder how they even got up to this cave to put in the door? Maybe the aliens put it in."

The tomb raider kept putting one chalked hand in front of the other as she ascended the steep face of the mountain, anchoring her rope as she went. Her rented Wrangler looked like nothing more than a blue shadow far below her feet. It was only thirty more feet to the cave.

A stiff breeze blew, and Shay took a deep breath. She didn't fear heights, but her stomach tightened when she looked down.

Shay reached the cave's ledge and pulled herself up and over.

Good news is at least the climb down will be easier. Thanks, gravity, for not always being a bitch.

She stood and activated her headlamp before striding into the cave. A few feet in she stopped, frowning.

Condensed moisture coated the rocks. She'd seen it with her drone, but she hadn't considered the implications. Where there was water there was usually life, and she didn't see a single mushroom or strand of moss. Maybe there were toxins or heavy metals in the rock, or residual alien radiation from centuries prior.

"Should start bringing a Geiger counter, too."

Shay frowned as she came up to the door. She took a deep breath and placed her palm on the flat panel. Nothing happened.

Guess it's not some ancient alien panel, or if it is, it's looking for something I don't have. Time to try this the old-fashioned way and hope this shit will open.

She pushed on the door, and the bottom scraped against the cave floor. At least it hadn't been locked. With the aid of her shoulder and a little grunting, the door swung open.

The headlamp revealed a vast cavern choked with long stalagmites and stalactites, almost as if she were inside the jaw of a monstrous stone beast pretending to be a mountain. Unlike the outer cave, the irregular shape of much of the chamber didn't suggest anything unusual. She'd gone from unnatural to natural-but-unnerving.

Soft dripping and running water echoed from a narrow passageway at the back of the cavern.

Shay didn't move for a couple of minutes as she continued sweeping the room for any sign of enemies or traps with both her headlamp and the IR and UV modes of her goggles. Nothing. Empty. No humans, no demons. Not even any bugs.

She chuckled.

Sometimes it's more about just finding the damned place. At least it's a nice change of pace.

Satisfied with the lack of any killer ancient alien laser death traps or scaly demons, the tomb raider maneuvered through the maze of stalactites and stalagmites to the passageway. The sloping path took her forty feet down and into another chamber.

A deep, cloudy pool of algae-infested water filled the center of the room, the source of which was water steadily dripping from several holes in the wall. The running water noise she'd heard before emanated from the walls above her—a hidden stream.

That mystery was of minor interest. The more obnoxious find was the lack of other exits, or anything looking like the artifact or a container.

Shay stared at the pool of water and groaned. "There's no way I'm lugging a stupid aquatic drone all the way up here."

She moved closer to the pool and shined the light into it, but the thick algae blocked any attempts to plumb its depths. She switched to IR mode, but couldn't spot any major thermal differentials in the water.

"You've got to be fucking kidding me."

Over the next couple of minutes, Shay removed all gear that couldn't take a little water. Bile rose in her throat at the idea of swimming through a slime-infested pool in the middle of a cave.

On the other hand, If I ended up dying because of some brain-eating amoeba rather than some asshole shooting me, it'd be kind of funny.

Shay finished by removing her holster and tactical harness and grabbed a single adamantine knife. She didn't expect to find anything in the water, but she didn't want to end up dying because some random underwater plant snagged her leg.

She moved to the edge of the pool and took several deep breaths. "Yeah, gonna have to shower five times when I get back to Quito to feel clean after this."

Shay closed her eyes and dove into the pool. She kicked with her legs to dive straight down, her free palm out. The slimy bottom of the pool turned out to be only eight feet down.

The thick algae coated her exposed skin as she pushed through the water. She shuddered under the light touch of the plants and didn't dare open her eyes.

Fumbling around with her hand, she felt along the bottom of the pool. Thirty seconds passed without finding anything more than rocks. A minute.

Shay shot up, breaking the surface and taking a deep lungful of air. Her disgusting first trip had given her nothing, but she'd only explored a small portion of the pool.

"Okay, attempt number two."

Six tries later her hand passed over something angled and smooth, but her burning lungs forced her back up before she could get a good hold on the object.

Shay tossed her knife into the pile with the rest of her gear and returned to the spot in the center of the pool. Using both hands, she felt along the edges of the suspicious object, which was clearly some sort of metal box. She braced her feet, and with a mighty tug, she freed the box.

Once back at the surface, she dared opened her eyes. A smooth golden box with a hinged lid rested in her hands. She swam to the edge of the pool and climbed out, a stupid grin on her face.

"Now let's see if all that disgusting swimming was worth it."

Shay turned on her headlamp and lifted the lid, and something gold shone under the light—a small figurine, a thick golden triangle with two long connected wings and what might charitably be interpreted as two tail fins, rested inside. The Bomber.

Up close, the figurine didn't strike the tomb raider as looking all that close to an aircraft, but it didn't resemble any animal she'd ever seen either.

Of course, the artisans might have just been making something cool.

Shay shrugged and gathered her gear. She'd get paid whether it was the key to an ancient alien mystery or a nice toy for the emperor's kid. Before she handed it over to the client, she'd perform a thorough examination and take some pictures.

Other than the whole swimming through muck thing, this wasn't so bad.

The small chamber shook, and a loud bellowing groan echoed around her.

"Now what?"

22

Stray rocks shook loose from the walls and roof of the small chamber, pelting the ground and splashing into the pool. The shaking stopped, but a dark shadow moving in the pool made the tomb raider's heart pound.

Yeah, that's what I get for thinking it'd be so easy.

She yanked out her gun and backed toward the passageway leading to the next chamber. Water splashed all over the room as something leapt out of the pool with a screech.

Shay's headlamp illuminated the slick and scaly body of a tall humanoid creature. It was more lizardman than demon, having glowing red eyes and long sharp claws. The monster hissed as he landed.

"You don't have to die here," Shay yelled, "but I'm not going to either. Back the fuck off."

The lizardman charged, and Shay's three shots echoed in the small chamber. The lizardman jerked back and dropped to the ground, his wounds spewing glowing blue blood. Shay put two more bullets into his head to be sure.

"Okay, that wasn't so bad."

Several additional dark forms appeared in the pool.

"Shit. This is what I get for not bringing a grenade on the climb."

Shay spun and rushed through the passageway. Red eyes and hisses followed her from the darkness. She unloaded her magazine into the darkness. Two loud screeches followed.

The tomb raider maneuvered between the dense stalagmites and stalactites choking the next chamber. A claw sliced at her from the side, from a lizardman hiding in the shadows. She ducked, whipped her gun up, and pulled the trigger.

Click. Empty.

Fuck.

Four more enemies lumbered from the darkness, snapping mouths filled with razor-sharp teeth and brandishing their claws.

Let's see how sharp my babies are.

Shay dropped the gun and yanked out an adamantine knife for each hand. She rushed the closest lizardman and slammed a blade into his head. The monster collapsed in a spray of glowing blue.

The tomb raider stayed low and darted between the mineral formations, slashing with both knives at two closing lizardmen. Her blades dug deeply, but didn't finish the creatures off. Both screeched and stepped back.

At least now I know these things understand fear. I can work with that.

"That's right, you ugly assholes. Don't fuck with me if you want to leave this cave alive."

More screeches and hisses sounded from the passageway.

"How many of you things were hiding in here?"

An unwounded lizardman leapt at her. She met his throat with a knife, but his claws ripped into her, slicing through her shirt and undershirt. Shay hissed as pain lanced through her side, warm blood welling up from the wound.

The two enemies she'd wounded earlier pressed a new attack. Both charged her, but their movements were unsteady and their glowing blood dripped to the ground. Shay met their charge by thrusting knives into their chests, and they screeched and thrashed for a few seconds before slumping to the ground.

Guess their hearts are in the right place. Lucky me.

Shay hurried through the chamber, not willing to risk the time to try to find her lost gun in the darkness. She had several reserve guns in her vehicle—assuming she didn't get torn to pieces before returning to it.

Her footfalls echoed as she bolted toward the thankfully-open golden door. More lizardmen boiled from the passage behind her, their screeches and hisses forming a dissonant choir.

Do they have a whole fucking city hidden under this cave or something?

The tomb raider rushed toward the mouth of the cave, her side throbbing from her earlier wound. She was hours away from Quito, and had only a single healing potion in the back of the Wrangler. If their claws carried any sort of venom or toxin, her agonizing death might soon await.

Shay shook her head. She needed to concentrate on escaping.

Rappelling back to the base of the mountain without proper safety precautions when she was already wounded wasn't one of Shay's better ideas, but she'd rather die quickly from falling than be torn apart by a horde of angry lizardmen.

"Here goes nothing."

Shay slid into the harness and anchored a rope as quickly as she could, feeding the rope through the carabiner before she leapt off the edge. "Don't look at the dog that's chasing you," she said between clenched teeth.

Pain in her side pulsed in time with her heart as she started her descent. A half-dozen lizardmen stood on the ledge, staring down at her with their red eyes as they hissed and screeched. They waved their claws.

"Damn, half-wish you guys would have run off the edge." She gave them a little salute. "But I have to go now."

The tomb raider continued making her way down the mountain, but the dark forms above didn't retreat to the cave. Nothing but her car awaited below, so she wasn't sure why they were waiting.

Hoping I just fall to my death, assholes? Good luck with that. I've been hurt way worse than this and escaped from much smarter killers than you.

Shay's breaths came out shallow and ragged. Her side was on fire, but she had hundreds more feet to go. The pain focused her awareness on her body and the descent, the cave's guardians pushed to a small corner of her mind.

It was time to solve the immediate problem before moving to something else.

The Wrangler had started as a distant blur before growing into a flat angular shape. The minutes passed, and suddenly it looked three-dimensional again.

Sweet, sweet ground lay only a few feet below her.

Shay dropped from the rope with a hiss, unhooking herself from the anchor and stumbled to the back of the vehicle. She opened the back hatch and grabbed the first-aid kit to apply an analgesic spray. A long sigh of relief followed. Some pain remained, but at least the fire had been extinguished.

Slumping against the vehicle, she lifted her shirt to assess the extent of the wound. Deep lacerations lined her side. If she hadn't had a healing potion, she would have needed stitches, in addition to a risk of infection.

Underestimated the raid just because I got here and didn't see anyone. Damn it.

Shay took out the potion from her first-aid kit. She'd wanted to keep it for a worst-case scenario, but there was no way she could risk the bumpy ride back down the mountain without taking care of the wound first.

Shay uncorked the bottle and downed the sour-tasting contents. Her wounds knitted themselves closed over the next thirty seconds, and the residual pain left. Another sigh of relief followed.

After a deep breath, the tomb raider stared up toward the ledge. It was too far now to make out any details in the thickening mist. The guardians might still be waiting, or they might have started down the side of the mountain. Waiting here to go another round didn't appeal.

With her heart slowing and her wounds taken care of, Shay's water-soaked clothes weighed on her body, and their earthy, rotten stench turned her stomach.

She reached into her pocket. The Bomber rested comfortably inside. She'd found what she'd come for. There was no reason to stay.

"See you around, lizard assholes. If it's any consolation, at least no one has a reason to come here anymore."

Shay wrapped her hair in a towel and put on a fluffy terrycloth robe. A forty-five-minute shower might be excessive under normal circumstances, but she wanted to ensure she eradicated any hint of the smell of the cave water in her nostrils. Even after her shower, the slimy feel of the algae lingered.

Ugh, that was nasty. Next time I should bring a cargo drone and ferry some equipment up first in case I need it.

She laughed. Next time? She'd gotten out of the hitman business because she had worried about dying young and being forgotten, but she wasn't so sure that being a hitman wasn't safer than being a tomb raider.

In her career, she'd already faced, among other things, ghosts, lizardmen, witches, mercenaries, frog-men, the world's strongest wand, and an invisible army. Being a tomb raider meant being shoved into the middle of dangerous locations to seek out powerful artifacts.

I'm not gonna die in my kitchen. I'm gonna die in some musty cave in the middle of nowhere, and no one will find my body for decades, if not centuries.

Shay stared at herself in a mirror for a moment. For whatever reason, the idea didn't scare her. The plan remained the same—save money and retire—but tomb raiding filled her with satisfaction that went beyond a job well done.

She was pushing into dark history long since lost, uncovering truth. Sure, sometimes that truth ended up in some asshole's private gallery, but better there than under hundreds of feet of water or in a destroyed ruin.

The only question she couldn't answer was how long she could do the job. Years? Decades? The original plan had an end goal, but no real timeline. Given all the money she'd already saved, she could probably retire tomorrow if she wanted to.

But I just don't want to. Fuck it, a little danger plus history makes for a nice spice. Not like James couldn't retire either.

I'll sip drinks on a beach when I'm old and broken. For now, I still have a lot of asses to kick and artifacts to find.

Shay stepped out of the bathroom and smiled down at the Bomber, which sat on a nightstand near her hotel bed. Although the room had a safe, she didn't trust it to hold something so valuable. Once she got her new clothes, she'd keep the artifact on her person until she turned it over to the client's representative back in the States.

Her phone rang, and she hurried to the bed to pick it up. Peyton. She'd sent him a quick text once she'd gotten a signal on her phone again, but she'd left out the details about getting sliced up by lizardmen. The man wouldn't be able to resist some horrible joke about the job.

"What's up?" Shay answered. "Client whining or something?"

"Nope. Have I ever told you how awesome I am?"

Shay snorted. "Yeah, lots of times. What about it?"

"I've got good news, or maybe bad news depending on how you look at it. But I think you'll believe it's good news."

"What's the damned news?"

"Durand's in Quito right now. He should have just landed."

Shay grinned. "Did he now?"

"Yep. I've spent the entire time you've been gone trying to track him, and I got lucky. Well, not lucky. I'm awesome still, but... Anyway, he's in Quito. Thought you might want to know."

"Thanks, Peyton. That *is* good news."

"See? Knew it."

"I'll take it from here. I'm gonna have a little fun with our favorite Frenchman, but I'll be on a flight home tomorrow morning."

"See you then."

Shay hung up and smirked.

Too damned late, Durand.

Shay strolled toward the tree-flanked patio of the cozy restaurant. The colorful tables were filled with chatting customers happily eating a glorious array of mouthwatering food; empanadas, soups, fruit, fried plantains, and ceviche.

Her stomach rumbled, but she didn't care about getting a snack or breakfast. She only cared about the blond man sitting at a table near the corner, his back to the wall and a bowl of soup in front of him.

Good for you, Durand. Nice defensive seating. Too bad about everything else.

The retrieval specialist might have been better on the ground in DC and Russia, but she'd been ahead of him from the start this time. It'd been pathetically easy to find the man. He might be a ghost electronically, but a few bribes to the local underworld representatives had gotten Shay his location within hours. He stood out in Ecuador, as did she, but she was more than willing to splash enough cash around to earn some assistance, and her proficiency in the language helped.

Durand folded his hands in front of him and wore a mocking smile on his face as if he'd been expecting her. Maybe he didn't want her to think he was about to shoot her. She kept her hands visible to communicate the same, even though she had knives strapped to her thighs beneath her dress and a gun in her purse. Becoming a fugitive in Ecuador wouldn't help her.

I'll make you wipe that shit-eating grin off your face. You don't know how badly I've beaten you, asshole.

Shay sat across from him with a grin. "No goons today? I'm disappointed. Who's gonna wipe your ass for you?"

"Sometimes I need assistants, but often I don't. I'm sure you'll agree that it's often better to work alone."

"It makes for fewer variables."

Durand nodded. "Exactly, and the kind of men you can get on short notice with money aren't always the most trustworthy."

"Says the mercenary."

"I'm not a mercenary, I'm a retrieval specialist. We're no different, Aletheia. You work for clients who pay you. I do the same thing."

"Bullshit. I have standards, and I'm not all about burying the truth, unlike your asshole bosses."

Durand shrugged. "The truth always comes out eventually, doesn't it? Oriceran is proof of that. Anything you or I do with regards to artifacts doesn't matter in the long run."

"You're such a cheerful guy."

"I consider myself a realist."

"I'm more of a pessimist, myself."

Shay appropriated his glass of water, took a sip, and set the glass down. "Now it's half empty." She frowned. "You don't seem surprised to see me, Durand."

"Disappointed?"

"A little, but I've still got a few tricks up my sleeve."

"I see. What you have to understand is that when I arrived few took notice of me, but this morning many local scum started shadowing me. It was too obvious. The local criminals aren't very good at staying out of sight. It inconvenienced me since I had to lose several tails, but it was minor, I assure you." He sighed. "If that was your grand revenge, it's pathetic."

"Maybe they tagged you as a rich asshole they could rob. You have to admit you have a very punchable face."

"No. It was as if they had all learned who I was, which made me think." Durand tapped his temple. "There are very few people who know who and what I am. There are even fewer who seek the same types of artifacts. It wasn't difficult after that to figure out that you were looking for me, Aletheia." He swirled his spoon in his soup bowl. "Rookie mistake. Too bad."

Shay snorted. "I'll give you this… You might piss me off, but you're not a complete fucking moron. That's more than I can say for a lot of the assholes I've run into in this job."

The Frenchman barked a laugh. "Ah, such sweet words from such a beautiful woman. We don't have to be enemies, you know. We could…be something far more pleasurable." His eyebrows lifted suggestively.

If we weren't on a patio in Ecuador, I'd so lay your ass out.

Shay rolled her eyes. "Don't ruin the compliment by trying to be slick, asshole. I'd sooner swim through a muck-infested pool and fight lizardmen than do anything with you."

Durand pushed his bowl of soup to the side. "Then, what now? Did you come to threaten me away from the artifact? Was that your brilliant plan?"

"You know, I'm glad you're here, actually. I would have been sad if you hadn't shown up."

"Oh? You made your personal feelings clear already." He frowned. "If you're going to offer some feeble professional alliance, don't bother. I don't need the help of a rookie, Aletheia. I haven't killed you out of professional courtesy, but don't assume my charity is infinite."

Shay shook her head and leaned forward, her voice dropping as she spoke. "Listen to you…so full of yourself. No, I didn't come here to ask for an alliance, and I'm glad you're here because it confirms the artifact is some alien shit and not just a neat little golden toy. It makes a lot of what I've gone through worth it. Well, the million dollars will, too."

Durand's smile faltered for a second. "Leave Quito now. If you go after the artifact, I can't guarantee your safety."

"You don't get it, do you?" Shay flipped him off. "Guess what, asshole? I already got it. You were too damned slow."

His mouth twitched. "You think you can fool me with such obvious lies?"

The tomb raider lifted her bright orange purse and set it on the table. She pulled it open, revealing the Bomber comfortably stowed in a vacuum-sealed bag.

Durand snorted. "Your arrogance is impressive. You really think I won't kill you and take this?"

"You're gonna kill me in public?"

"Most people are weak. They'll scatter the minute I go for my gun."

"And you don't think I'll go for mine?"

"I've already proven that you can't surprise me in DC, and now here."

Oh, this is gonna be good.

"Really?" Shay nodded to one side and then the other. Two pairs of large men in jeans and T-shirts sat a few tables down, their hands and guns hidden underneath the table. They frowned at Durand.

"Guess you were wrong about the quality of our local creepers," Shay suggested. "Yeah, sometimes it's good to work alone, but sometimes it's good to hire a little local help. The kind of guys who really know the streets, you know?" She closed the purse and pulled it over her shoulder. "Here's how this is gonna go, Durand. I'm gonna get up and walk away. If you try to do anything, the nice gentlemen I paid a large sum of money to for *protection* will shoot you, or at a minimum, distract you long enough that *I* can shoot you. I might end up dead, but there's no way this doesn't end with *you* dead if you try something. Mutually-assured destruction, asshole."

Durand sneered. "Why bother with this farce? Why didn't you pay them to kill me in my room?"

"You're too good to get taken out by local thugs if you're on your game. I knew this would only work if I gave you something shiny to focus on." Shay pointed to her chest. "Like me." She scooted her chair back and stood. "It's been fun, Durand, but I've got an artifact to deliver to a client." Her smile vanished. "Who's the fucking rookie now, douchebag?"

Shay waved and stepped away from the table.

Two days later, Shay hummed as she reclined on a love seat in her living room. The delivery had gone smoothly, and she'd made sure to take pictures from various angles.

Look at me, humming? Satisfied and happy. Definitely gonna make James take me to a nice Italian place soon. Have a real date.

The tomb raider was now a million dollars richer and had gotten a nice boost to her reputation. She might not be willing to admit it to Peyton, but he'd been right. The job had soothed her ego after Russia, and her only regret was that she hadn't taken a picture of the look on Durand's face when he realized she'd outsmarted him.

So, what to do with some of my time off?

A little routine might not be bad. Going out running with Free-to-Move, maybe weekly dancing nights with the girls between tomb raids.

A life. When Shay had burned down her house she'd

been running from what she thought was a life, but it had been an empty shell, devoid of real relationships or connections. That was why it'd been so easy to fake her death and walk away without ever looking back.

Her phone buzzed and she grabbed it, expecting Peyton or James. The text was from neither man.

NOT UNDERWOOD: I need to speak to you about a matter of mutual interest. I need you to come to me, but I won't make you run all the way to DC.

Time and address followed in a separate text.

"What the fuck? That's in an hour."

Shay groaned and scrubbed a hand over her face. Correk might be the Fixer, but he wasn't her boss. She didn't like the idea of jumping whenever he snapped his fingers.

"Shit," she murmured. "If he's contacting me, it's not gonna be for a friendly chat."

Shay rose from the couch and grumbled.

"This is why I shouldn't even bother trying to establish a routine."

Shay pulled her Spider into an open parking spot on the street. This was the right address, but she didn't see Correk. Several small restaurants and bars lined the street, and chatting people walked the sidewalks.

"Which damned building is it?"

She pulled her phone out of her pocket and clicked on her text messages to review Correk's. There'd been a date, time, and address when the message was sent, but it'd disappeared. Apparently, in Correk's Fixer library, there was a spell to make any text chat appear in an updated version of Snapchat.

"Cute, Correk." She texted him.

I'm here. Where am I supposed to go?

Keep looking and you'll find it.

"Thanks for the cryptic comment." She gritted her teeth. "Elves."

Shay stepped out of her car and looked around for anything obvious. She spotted an elf walking by himself. While not the only elf in the streams of pedestrians, he was the only one not dressed for a night on the town.

He turned a corner and slipped between two buildings. She sprinted across the street when it was clear and headed toward the elf's last location.

When Shay turned the corner, she didn't see anything but windows and a few stray wrappers lying on the ground.

"Disappeared?"

She spun around, half-expecting the elf to show up behind her like Durand in DC, but there was no one. The tomb raider turned slowly as she sought evidence of a hidden door.

Something was wrong. Shay shook her head and turned back and forth again, this time counting as she moved her eyes.

1...2...3...*Wait.*

Her eyes moved too quickly on one side. She focused where she'd been looking, and after a few seconds and a blink there was a narrow door.

Fucking magic.

Shay narrowed her eyes as she stared at the nondescript door. It took all her concentration for her gaze not to slide away and ignore it.

Fucking hate that type of spell. I swear, Correk, if this thing ends up wiping my memory, I will find you and kick your Fixer ass.

Shay took a few deep breaths and marched straight toward the door. The more she let her thoughts stray, the harder it was to keep her gaze on the entrance, but finally she pulled it open and stepped inside.

Darkness reigned, and strange smells floated through the air, some acrid, others fruity or herbal. Floating orbs provided light near the tables and the bar.

Magical light. Magical defensive spell. Huh.

A light-colored wooden bar ran along the back of the room. A Light Elf bartender dressed in a black silk shirt, and tie stood behind the bar with a smile on his face. Shelves containing dozens of bottles were behind him. Most appeared to be Earth alcohol, but others were labeled in Oriceran languages or glowing concoctions that obviously hadn't been distilled in Kentucky. A row of stoppered and differently-colored small glass bottles, most likely potions, were on the top shelf.

A few people glanced her way before returning to their conversations and drinks.

Definitely not your average sports bar.

Numerous elves sat in the bar, and a few dwarves huddled in a corner. One of the dwarves puffed on a long pipe, eyeing her for a moment.

A gnome sat at the bar pounding back an opaque green drink. Judging by the wands hanging from belts or peeking out of coats, most of the people who looked human were witches or wizards.

Two women with wings were at a table in a corner giggling over some video they were watching on a phone. Shay assumed they were Arpaks, but she'd never seen one up close.

Correk waved from a table in the center of the room. A wine glass sat in front of him.

At least he's not drinking some weird glowing Oriceran thing.

Shay wasn't happy that the Fixer had taken the least defensible seat in the entire room, but given the magical nature of the place, she doubted she had to worry about some rogue cartel survivor kicking in the door and shooting her in the back.

That would be kind of fun to see, but I'm not here for that.

The tomb raider slid into a seat with a grunt.

Been spending too much time around James. She snickered.

"Maybe next time you can give me a little more lead time for the meeting," Shay suggested.

Correk shrugged. "I apologize. I don't always have…a predictable schedule, so I meet with people when I can." He offered her a faint pained smile.

"Whatever. I'm assuming it's important. I'm guessing you didn't call me out here to drink gnome grog."

"Yes, and let me thank you for being on time, Miz Carson," Correk told her. He took a sip of his wine. "That makes the rest of my night far less stressful. I'm glad you were able to find the place."

"You didn't tell me about the spell."

"I *did* tell you to keep looking."

"But you didn't tell me about the spell to begin with."

Correk's eyes narrowed. "Consider it another test of your abilities. If you couldn't find this place, you probably wouldn't be worth working with."

"Ouch. You still don't think I have what it takes?"

"I think it didn't hurt to check. We're swimming together in mysterious waters. I need to be assured that you have a flexible mind."

Shay rolled her eyes.

Correk put his wine glass down after taking another sip. "I've spent a long time dealing with dangerous magic and dangerous people. I've gained valuable allies along the way, such as Smite-Williams and Lei—" He sucked in a breath. "Other people, but I'm still deciding whether you're a valuable ally or someone who'll cause trouble because you know just enough to be dangerous."

"Maybe I'm a dangerous ally."

The elf chuckled. "Always a possibility, but I trust you're satisfied with how I've tested you."

"Maybe I'll test *you* next time."

Correk smirked. "Trust me, I can make it through the As Seen on TV aisle without trouble."

Shay blinked, not following the elf's logic but decided to let it drop. She wasn't there to trade jokes anyway. "So, what's the deal with this place? Some secret magic bar? I don't get it. It's not like Oricerans can't drink in human bars."

"Sure, but human bars are filled with humans."

"That they are." Shay pointed to herself. "I'm human, you know."

"Let me be very clear. I'm not anti-human, it's just that the bulk of humanity is still coming to terms with the full return of magic, and that can cause complications in my duties as the Fixer." Correk gestured around the bar. "As for this place, in addition to the spells the owners put on the bar, I know I can use certain spells here without a problem. I wanted to make sure that no other humans overheard our conversation. As you've noted, you're human, but you already are deep into the investigation. I'm more concerned about the government people looking into this matter. I don't trust them, and I've had bad experiences with human governments before when it comes to sensitive matters."

Shay snorted. "Not like most humans trust our governments either. You don't have to convince me. I barely trust myself, and..." She furrowed her brow, wondering how much she should share.

"What is it?"

"I ran into a man working for the US government in Ecuador just a few days ago. They've got this specialist, Francois Durand. He's been running all over grabbing alien-related shit. He's probably the guy who got them their stone. He was in Ecuador to grab something that might have been alien-related."

Correk arched a brow. "Really?"

"Yeah. I was recovering an artifact down there for a client. It was a little golden airplane-looking thing, but it was six hundred years old. Ancient airplanes, allegedly, or models of them, anyway."

He nodded. "I'm familiar with them."

"I took a bunch of pictures in different spectral ranges, but I couldn't find anything unusual about it. No symbols, nothing. If it's related to the aliens, it might be indirect. Or maybe it's what people think it is: just something the Incas made after seeing alien aircraft."

"Where is it now?"

"With the client."

Correk frowned. "I see."

"Hey, the guy paid a million dollars for it, and it wasn't covered with alien glyphs or anything."

"I have ways of recovering information that go beyond simple reading and translation. In the future, it could be helpful to our investigation if I could gain access to an artifact like that, if only for a short while."

"Understood." Shay stared at the Light Elf, wondering how much information she should offer.

Have to give a little to get a little. I'm not gonna get better help than the Fixer.

Shay sighed. "This Durand asshole beat me to an artifact in Russia. An aluminum tooth-wheel that may be three hundred million years old, so it's got to be alien."

"I see." Correk picked up his wine and downed the rest of it. "I presume this item is now under the control of the American government?"

Shay shrugged. "As far as I know. This Durand guy might not be a Fixer, but he's damned good for a human with no special magic. He's gonna be a problem, but I'll deal with him when he pops up."

Correk set his glass down and folded his hands in front of him. "I thank you for being so honest about the information you've uncovered, Miz Carson. Since you've been so forthright, I will be as well."

"Oh, you didn't call me here to hit on me?"

Correk gave a soft snort. "Don't think so highly of yourself."

She rolled her eyes. "You're no fun."

"No, I'm not—not when it comes to my duties." Correk made a few precise movements with his hand while he sang, or at least that was the closest word that Shay could use to describe it. What emerged from his mouth wasn't a simple voice, but a complex, layered sound that should have required instruments.

A full-color three-dimensional image of a pitted and cracked rock winked into existence above the table. It rotated slowly.

"Do you know what this is?" Correk inquired.

"Looks like a rock to me."

"Close enough. It's a meteorite."

"You mean, it's a space rock."

Correk chuckled. "Yes."

Shay nodded. "Something special about meteorites? Sky iron or something like that for powerful magical metalworking?"

"More to the point, there's something special about this *particular* meteorite. A magical gentleman I helped out of a difficult situation gave it to me recently. He'd had it in his family for thousands of years, along with a family legend about it being a blessing stone from an ancient god."

"Huh. Any way to verify that?"

"Partially. Being the Fixer does have its advantages. I've examined this meteorite using various powerful spells, and I've determined several important things. It is indeed a meteorite, and it has magical biological residue on it."

He moved his hand, and glowing green lines appeared on the meteorite image.

Shay tilted her head as she examined the lines. "Was this some sort of attack, or a colonize-the-Earth-with-alien-spores thing?"

"I can't be sure, but I don't believe so." Correk shook his head. "There are limits to even *my* magic, but I was able to determine this was part of a burial of some sort. A funeral offering. I was also able to verify that this meteorite doesn't originate on Earth or Oriceran, but it was discovered on Earth."

"Okay, so our boys had an interstellar Viking funeral. That's not a super-concern, not that I don't want to dig deeper."

The elf waved his hand, and the image rotated to reveal several symbols. Shay's heart rate kicked up. She didn't recognize most of them, but one had already been seared into her brain as she spent hours looking at it on a picture of James' amulet.

So, he is linked to all this shit. Damn. That means that Durand asshole might start snooping around him eventually.

No, wait. It's fine. He doesn't wear it where people can see it. There's no way the government will ever know to go after him as long as I keep him far away from all this shit.

Shay forced a smile. Exchanging information with Correk didn't mean he needed to know everything. For all she knew, the Fixer might decide that James was a threat who needed to be eliminated. The less he knew about James Brownstone, the better.

Correk gestured toward the image. "When we talked

before, you mentioned translating the phrase 'Already here.'"

"Yeah, that's all my people have been able to ascertain, but you said we didn't know what that means. That it could mean all sorts of things."

"True, but you've mentioned six-hundred-year-old arti-facts and three-hundred-million-year-old artifacts. The stone you collected for the Professor wasn't that ancient, but it was still very, very old."

"Yeah? I sense a 'but' coming."

Correk pointed at the spinning meteorite. "This mete-orite is mere decades old, not thousands or millions."

"Shit."

"Indeed. I'm glad you appreciate the implications." The elf flicked his wrist, and the image vanished. "So, *they*, whoever they are, are already here. They came here some time ago, and I believe they're still here."

Shay exhaled slowly. "But who are 'they,' exactly?"

Is there some other person like James out there? Even if there is, everyone would just assume they are magical. Or maybe James was sent here to escape them?

Correk frowned. "I'm not totally sure. My analysis tells me they possess some unique abilities. They leave a trail like magic, but it's not quite magical." He shook his head. "I honestly can't be sure. The only thing I *can* be sure of is that Earth is a lot more interesting than anyone on Earth or Oriceran realizes."

Shay leaned back in her chair with a frown. "If the government has any clue about this, it would explain why they've hired people like Durand. This isn't some history lesson to them. They might be thinking there's an invasion going on."

"And they might be right. It's not like Earth and Oriceran have a monopoly on evil people."

"Or it might be nothing, or just a few alien tourists."

James isn't a fucking invader. A crying and scared kid doesn't invade a planet, but maybe he was a mistake? Maybe his parents were supposed to come with him. A bunch of amulet-wearing assassins might be running around planning to take out all the major world leaders, for all I know.

Shay shook her head. She couldn't be sure of anything other than that she would protect James from both Correk and himself if necessary.

I guess this is what love is—protecting your alien boyfriend from some Light Elf responsible for helping all magical beings on a planet.

Fuck, this is complicated!

"It doesn't matter what the truth is," Correk commented softly. "It only matters what the government believes."

"That's what you think the government is really trying to stop?"

"Yes. Good luck kicking out the actual aliens."

24

S hay kept both hands on the wheel as she pulled away from the meeting, every muscle in her body tense. She'd originally gotten involved in the alien mess only because of some chance information Peyton had found about a missing tomb raider.

Alien invasions? Ancient aliens who aren't so ancient, and somehow James is wrapped up in all this. What the hell?

She didn't know what to believe about the strange elf she'd fought in Mexico. She wasn't sure if he was an alien-infested host body or a demon who wanted to find an alien planet to invade. Maybe he was just a nutty elf.

No, that couldn't be true, not totally. The stone was a genuine alien artifact, and Project Nephilim and Project Ragnarok were both interested in the alien stones. The government wouldn't be spending piles of money and hiring elite retrieval specialists if there wasn't something real.

Shay sighed. "And here I thought faking my death and

shifting from being a hitman to a tomb raider would be the most complicated shit I had to worry about."

Was she doing the right thing by keeping the rest of the truth from James? The man was finding a bit of peace after years of being alone in his relationships with both her and Alison. His issues handling emotions made more sense now that she understood his true background.

No. Fuck it. James can't do anything about it. This is a job for a tomb raider and a Fixer, not a bounty hunter, even if he's the toughest fucking bounty hunter on this planet. He doesn't need the fucking stress.

Shay yanked on the wheel, taking a hard turn at an intersection. She'd protect her man, no matter what she needed to do. She might not be an alien, but giving a shit about another person was as new to her as it was to James.

Her phone buzzed and she picked it up, expecting a text from Peyton or Correk. Instead, it was from an unknown number. The message was straightforward enough.

I understand you've been looking for me. I'm at Prophecy Gaming right now.

Shay snorted. "Oh, you're finally back in fucking town, Tubal-Cain? What is this, the official Oriceran Abrupt Meeting Night?"

The one thing Shay could say about the night was that finding Prophecy Gaming was far less annoying than it usually was. Maybe she was just getting better at concentrating and beating that redirection glamour.

Tubal-Cain sat in a chair and looked up at her expectantly, and Shay tossed a few pictures on the table in the backroom.

"What's this?"

"You wanted me to find your cousin. This is evidence I think might at least lead to him."

Several of the pictures were satellite photos of a nondescript farm, with a few other ground-level photos of the same boring-ass farm. One photo revealed the dozens of gnomes who were hidden from normal sight, the split-second image Peyton had ripped from the drone feed.

Shay didn't feel the need to inform the gnome how she'd set her assistant to the task, especially since she still had mixed feelings about the whole thing. Peyton leaving LA to go to Iowa hadn't been the smartest move, but she couldn't expect the man to hide his entire life. She hadn't even bothered to avoid Nuevo Gulf Cartel territory after faking her death, and they had been the reason for it.

Tubal-Cain leafed through the pictures. "A hidden gnome colony. That explains why my magic failed. So many gnomes gathered together requires extra security. Where is this place?"

"Iowa, not all that far outside Des Moines."

The gnome frowned. "Iowa. They could hide anywhere, but they chose Iowa?"

Shay shrugged. "Maybe they really like corn. What are they gonna do? Come to LA and enjoy our lovely smog?" She chuckled.

"I've never been to Iowa."

"I've been there before. Had an interesting time."

The gnome quirked a brow. "'Interesting time?'"

Shay waved a hand dismissively. "Don't worry about it. Just human stuff."

Yeah, admitting I offed a guy in the airport there won't make Tubal-Cain more comfortable with me.

"I'll need more information," the gnome explained. "Just knowing the general area isn't enough."

"No problem. I can get you coordinates, directions, and all that. Then you can go to the Hidden Valley of the Gnomes or whatever, but there's something you should know."

"What's that?"

Shay pointed at the photo containing the gnomes. "You didn't give us a description of your cousin, so we can't be a hundred percent certain he's there. I figure you can at least ask your buddies there if they've heard him, right?"

Tubal-Cain held up the photo and pointed to a gnome sitting at the end of a long table. "That's Bosvid right there. Looks exactly the same as the last time I saw him." He set the picture down, an odd look in his eyes. "I have to say I'm rather impressed, Miz Carson."

"I'm not exactly a rookie, Tubal-Cain." Shay snorted, imagining Durand sitting in the chair for a moment.

"Oh, by my standards, you're too inexperienced to even be worthy of a title like 'rookie.'"

Shay snorted. "Finding things is my business. You didn't think I was gonna be able to find the adamantine, and I did."

"True. I should stop underestimating you, human."

"Yeah, you should."

His gaze dropped to the photo. "But that doesn't change the fact that you found Bosvid when I couldn't."

Shay allowed herself a smirk. "Yeah, I did."

"You have my respect for that, Miz Carson. It couldn't have been easy."

Well, easy for me. I just told Peyton to do it.

"We discussed a little additional compensation."

The gnome nodded. "Yes, I believe we did."

Tubal-Cain stood and reached behind his back. He slowly pulled a velvet bag in front of him.

Shay blinked. "Where the hell did that come from?"

"Somewhere." He tossed the bag to her.

The tomb raider snatched the bag out of the air and looked inside. She blinked. "Uh, a paperclip? Seriously?"

Tubal-Cain cackled. "It's a magical lockpick. Bet you didn't think I could do it."

Shay shrugged. She didn't have doubts about his capabilities, but if the gnome wanted to think he was unpredictable, it wouldn't hurt to let him go on believing that.

He pointed toward the bag. "Simply unbend it and stick it in the lock. Say the incantation three times."

"Is this another weird gnome thing I have to memorize?"

"No. It's in your language this time. 'Open through will, open through heart, open through belief.' Do I need to write it down?"

"Might as well. Don't want to wake up tomorrow with a worthless magical lockpick." Shay smiled. "I appreciate this, Tubal-Cain. It will come in very handy on a lot of my jobs."

"Oh, I'm sure it will." He waggled a finger. "But I must warn you, Miz Carson…"

"What? Don't get it wet after midnight or something like that?"

The gnome shook his head. "This is a more powerful magical artifact than you realize. All magic is fickle and has rules. This is no exception."

"But you already told me the rules. Unbend it and use the incantation. What's the big deal?"

"No, that's how to use it. Those aren't the rules."

Why does magic have to be so fucking annoying? Living on Oriceran must be a nightmare.

Shay frowned. "What are the rules, then?"

"You'll find out, but the most important one is to remember that misuse has consequences. Use this item for darkness, and it will turn dark and eventually fail you."

"And turn me into a bird," Shay muttered, looking down.

"A bird? Maybe. Odd things happen, at least by human standards, when powerful magical artifacts are misused."

Shay sighed and looked back up. "But how will I know if I've...offended the lockpick? Do I chat with it or something?"

"You'll know. It'll tell you one way or the other." The gnome reached into his pocket and produced a hand-written note with the activation incantation. "Thank you, Miz Carson. I'm sure we'll have reason to do business again."

"I never doubted it."

25

The next morning Shay stopped for coffee at a small shop tucked next to her favorite old book store. There was a line, but it was steadily moving. Most people in line just wanted a large cup of black coffee so they could get back on the road.

Shay stood in line, not making eye contact with anyone in particular, doing a routine check of the crowd, inside and out. Just as she turned her head to the right she caught a glimpse of someone staring right at her before he quickly ducked out of view.

"Shit," she muttered, drawing a bored look from the man behind her. She immediately abandoned her place in line and rolled out of the shop, searching the street.

She had spotted a former New York City connection, an old rival who had almost as many professional kills as Shay, till she was presumed dead.

He had been close enough to get a good look at her face

and she saw the recognition in his eyes. She had to find him fast.

Shay glanced up at the windows above her and looked around as much as she dared, glancing down alleys. She saw him turning a corner at the end of an alley and she hesitated. It occurred to her he may be drawing her in further.

Make the kill, then let everyone know she *had* still been alive. *Think Shay, use your old skills. What would you do if you were the hunter instead of the prey?*

She peered out from the corner slowly, and as predicted a bullet whizzed too close to her head, barely making a noise. She pulled out her gun and tried again, getting off a shot before ducking back.

There wasn't a lot of time before someone would notice a gun battle between two well-dressed people with no camera crew in sight and call the cops. She turned around, ready to retreat and figure out a different option when she saw two thugs approaching from the other end. He had friends with him.

"Fuck me. I picked a bad moment to get stupid." A straight alley with only a few doors. She had to pray one of them was unlocked or that her parkour skills were greatly improved. and she could scale a building in a skirt.

Shay rolled to her right as the two men calmly raised their guns and she neatly picked off the one on the right, catching him in the shoulder and disabling his arm. Good enough for now. The other ducked behind a dumpster giving Shay a chance to look for an exit.

She pulled at the first door she got to and found it locked. Damn. Only two more to go. She turned and fired off another round, holding off one assailant as her old rival came around from the other side.

These are my last fucking seconds. Brownstone. Shay felt a surge of anger. *Not going out, just when things got to be good.* She pivoted shooting first in one direction and then the other, jiggling the second door. Nothing.

She heard the sound of a loud crow overhead as she reached for the third door. Faces appeared over the edge of the buildings, pelting the gunman behind the dumpster with rocks and small, glowing fireballs. At the front of the crowd Shay saw the long gray hair. "Lily," she whispered.

The gunman stood, trying to get off a shot at the teenagers on the rooftops, giving Shay the opportunity she needed. A clean kill right through the head.

She turned, her finger already squeezing the trigger, certain it was going to be a close race. She had only a moment to aim, even as she was pressing her back against the wall, determined to keep her eyes open and see what was coming.

A well-aimed rock hit her old rival's arm in just the right place and his bullet nicked the top of her shoulder. Shay did him one better and her bullet passed cleanly through his neck. He instinctively reached up and pressed a hand against the gurgle, even as he dropped to his knees and fell back.

The teenagers came pouring off the top of the building, surrounding Shay as Lily pushed her way to the front.

"That was your rock, wasn't it?" asked Shay, her heart still pounding. "You got a premonition." Thank God for her twitch muscles.

"I saw it all, but I didn't know if I'd be able to change

the outcome." Lily's words came out in a rush. "I'm sorry I ran away. I needed to see my friends and I didn't know how to choose. There wasn't a way to be in both worlds. I want to be a tomb raider and help Peyton but…" It was the most she had ever said to Shay at one time. Just as quickly, she stopped talking and wrapped her arms around Shay's neck, squeezing tight.

Shay realized she was still holding up her gun and lowered it, hugging the girl back. "We need to get out of here," she whispered. "Dead bodies tend to attract law enforcement."

"I know a way," said a young man.

"Shay, this is Harry. He's kind of the leader of the band."

Shay finally took in a deep breath and put away her gun. "Fireballs and rocks? I thought you were all magical?"

Harry let out a snort as a ripple of laughter went through the crowd. "We all have weird magic. Kind of works, most of the time. Sometimes, all you need is a well-aimed rock."

"Old school. I like it."

"Come on," said Lily, "we have a way out of here. You good?"

"Yeah, I'm good. I'll have to get Peyton to erase the video cameras in the area but shouldn't be too big a task. He misses you, you know."

"I miss him too. Tell him, I'll be back soon." Lily led the way to another entrance to the tunnels, leading Shay through the maze, splashing through standing water in her good heels. She was still too relieved to still be breathing and to see Lily again to care. Shoes can be replaced.

She came out a mile down and pulled out her phone to

text Purity Cleaners. They could make a quick run through the alley if they hurried and clean up the mess. Her car would be waiting for her at a previously agreed location.

She put away her phone and hugged Lily. "You don't need to choose. You can do both. We'll work it out. Just come back."

Shay found her car waiting for her two blocks away from where she got out of the Uber. When she rolled into Warehouse Two, she was disappointed to not see Peyton. She wanted to tell him she saw Lily.

She'd thought he was finally through with his issues regarding showing up at a decent time.

They didn't exactly work in a normal office environment, but she needed him to be available and ready to work, especially now that they were racing against Project Nephilim and Project Ragnarok. A reliable assistant would assure both survived the next few years.

Why isn't your shit together, Peyton? I'm trying hard not to let the Empress of All Bitches out, so please don't force me to release her.

Shay frowned and poked her head in the office. Osiris sat in Peyton's chair, staring at the tomb raider. If it were possible for a cat's face to be described as surly, the orange tabby's fit.

The cat hissed.

Shay flipped the cat off. "Stop looking at me like I'm an intruder, cat. This is my building. I own it. Your master works for me, which means *you* technically work for me."

She threw her hands up. "And now I'm arguing with a cat. Love it. Such a great use of my time. Really."

Osiris meowed and hopped off the chair. The cat strutted past her like he was the owner of the building, and hissed once more before running under a table.

"You'd *better* run, you stupid animal," Shay muttered. She shook her head. "And this is why I hate pets."

The pleasant smell of pepperoni drifted from the pizza oven.

Shay blinked. "If he's cooking he must be around here somewhere, but does he really need to make pizzas in the morning?"

Peyton was, if anything, becoming more of a pizza freak than even her. She liked eating pizza, but cooking pizza? Not so much.

It took time and devotion to master the fine art of pizza-making, and she'd never found the time.

No. I didn't want to find the time. He's made the choice, and he's gotten better. My time's better spent learning parkour and history than pizza-making. Don't need the redundant skill set.

Peyton turned the corner from the hallway and waved. "Hey, Shay. Sorry. Was just in the bathroom."

It was hard to ignore the flour on the end of his nose. She didn't care. She was still alive with no new holes.

Shay pointed toward his face. "Do I even want to know what that's about?"

"What?"

"There's something on your nose."

Peyton rubbed the flour off with his hand.

"Do I want to know what that's about?" He pointed at

her shoulder and the stains on her shoes. "You taking on a side job before breakfast?"

"Something like that. I ran into Lily."

Peyton's face lit up. "Based on your clothes, did that go very well?"

"Well enough. Got a promise out of her to come back… under her terms."

"I really like that girl and her misfit magic act."

Shay gestured to his outfit, which consisted of Gucci loafers and Gucci skinny yellow jeans. "I get it. This one makes sense, for once. It's supposed to be an Italian theme."

Peyton beamed. "Exactly. See? I put a lot of thought into what I wear, but I don't think you always realize that."

"Oh, I realize it, but that's not the same thing as liking it or having the theme make any sort of sense." Shay chuckled. "And what was up with the flour on your nose? You practicing snorting drugs before you move on to coke or dust?"

Peyton laughed. "Nope. It's all about pizza. I've been working on flour and crust lately." He rubbed his hands together. "I found some new recipes and realized one of my issues is that all my ingredients aren't premium, so it's inspired me to change my strategy. The new Pizza King Peyton is all about premium."

"Premium?"

"Yeah, like the olive oil I was using before. The olive oil we get in America is a joke. I might as well just have used spit."

"That's a bit strong."

"Doesn't make it any less true."

"So what's your solution?"

Peyton smiled. "I had some shipped from Italy, along with several types of specialty flours."

"You really need several different types of flours for your pizza?"

"Yeah. Totally. Some flours work better for different types of pizza. I've been doing a lot of experiments to figure what goes with what, and I'm slowly learning." Peyton paced and gesticulated. "The thing is, the flour's the foundation of everything. A house with a bad foundation's going to collapse eventually, and a pizza with a bad foundation's not going to taste good. So, yeah, I need to find the perfect flour if I don't want crap pizza."

"No one wants crap pizza, but you're seriously gonna keep importing ingredients?"

Peyton waved a hand dismissively. "No, I'm not importing ingredients. I'm importing the key pieces of the foundation of a potential culinary masterpiece."

"Your hobby's getting expensive, but I guess it's cheaper than coke, heroin, or dust."

"There can be no compromise when it comes to pizza." Peyton grinned. "You taught me that."

"I haven't seen any Chicago-style abominations from you, so there is *some* hope."

The man stopped pacing. Shay began to wonder if he were even paying any attention to her.

Peyton looked up. "Sourcing quality ingredients are one thing, but that's just part of the puzzle. You can have the best ingredients in the world, after all, and still produce garbage pizza."

"And what's the other part, then, oh aspiring Pizza King?"

"Timing and patience." Peyton walked over to the pizza oven. "I was in too much of a hurry before. If you want a perfect crust, you need perfect dough. You need perfect flour for that, but even with that, you also need to give it proper time to rise."

"And that's what the nose flour was about?"

He nodded. "Exactly. I've been experimenting, and I've found that letting it rise most of the day makes for the best dough."

"Most of the day?"

Shay gave him an appreciative nod and whistled. The few times she'd made pizza, she hadn't put anywhere near the care Peyton was describing into the process. It was no surprise that she'd been unsatisfied with her efforts.

Peyton bobbed his head. "Yes, most of the day. But you have to be careful, or disaster can strike."

Shay laughed. "Disaster? It's just pizza. It's not going to explode. Even your worst efforts just tasted awful. They didn't poison me." She tapped her bottom lip. "Then again, you managed to set the warehouse on fire, so that could easily have been a disaster."

"That was the old me, not Pizza King Me." Peyton shook his head. "And I was talking about being careful with the dough. Avoiding taste disasters."

Shay crossed her arms. "How does a Pizza King avoid a taste disaster?"

Peyton lifted a finger. "By ensuring his dough doesn't overrise. It'll throw off the flavor and texture, so you have to keep an eye on it."

"So, in other words, you've spent a lot of time babysitting dough?"

"That's one way to look at it."

"And what way would *you* look at it, then?"

"I prefer to call it foundation monitoring."

Shay laughed. "Is this what you do all day when I'm not around? Just fuck around with pizza?"

"Not...all the time. I mean, I do other stuff."

Shay didn't mind, but she enjoyed poking Peyton.

Still, despite the horrors he'd unleashed in his first few attempts, he'd gotten damned good at making pizza, and it was a nice treat. Admitting that the pizza oven had been a good addition might be too much, but she wasn't going to complain when she was getting such good food with no effort on her part.

"Speaking of timing..." Peyton grabbed his wooden pizza paddle. "Looks like the pizza is ready."

"Smells good," Shay admitted. "*Very* good."

"I hope you're ready for ham and pineapple." He flourished the paddle like a sword.

"Do you want to die immediately, or should I stretch it out to make you suffer your crimes against pizza-kind?"

Peyton laughed and slipped the paddle under the pizza. He pulled it out, revealing pepperoni, just as Shay had smelled.

"That's what I thought," she commented.

He slid the pizza into a waiting tray. "Oh oh oh...I actually forgot the most important ingredient. The true foundation. The foundation under the foundation."

"What's that?"

"Water. You need the right water."

"And what's the right water? Distilled?"

Peyton mock gasped. "The Queen of Pizza doesn't know the answer to that question?"

Shay rolled her eyes. "I eat it, I don't make it. What water are you using, Pizza King?"

"I needed water from the homeland of true pizza, so I've been importing Neapolitan water."

Shay burst out laughing. "You actually flew in water from Italy?"

Peyton sniffed. "It's a small price to pay for quality pizza, and I stand by all my choices."

The delicious pepperoni scent saturated the air. The arrangement and density of the toppings were masterful. The thickness of the cheese was perfect.

Her stomach rumbled. If the pizza tasted as good as it smelled and looked, she might have to acknowledge Peyton as the true Pizza King. *Damn.* His understanding of the intricacies of the art at least qualified him for consideration for the position.

"Slice that bad boy up," Shay ordered. "All your fancy talk is nothing without a taste-test. We'll see how worthy you are of—"

The office computer screeched a klaxon, and Peyton ran into the office and dropped into his chair. His face scrunched in confusion and his fingers flew across the keyboard. Shay followed him in, annoyed and still hungry.

"Damn it," Peyton muttered under his breath.

"What the fuck is going on? If it's that fucking Frenchman, I'll fly to wherever he is right now and put fifteen fucking bullets in his head for messing up my morning."

Peyton shook his head and continued to type. "I wish it *were* Durand. At least then I wouldn't be so worried."

Shay threw up her hands. "I guess I should say it again, and maybe you'll answer. What the fuck is going on?"

"It's my brother's guys. They're...better than I thought. Or maybe he hired new guys. I don't know."

"Meaning what, exactly? How are they better than you thought?"

"They've bypassed a lot of my misdirects and proxy servers. They're getting closer, and..." An alarm popped up, a pleasant chime accompanying it. Peyton's eyes widened. "Oh, sonofabitch! You've got to be kidding me! Shit, shit, shit."

Shay crossed her arms. "Talk to me, Peyton. What the hell is going on? Are they through your defenses?"

"No, they aren't." Peyton scrubbed a hand over his face. "You see, I've got alerts set up on my name in addition to all the network defense stuff."

"And?"

Peyton looked over at Shay. "And I'm no longer dead."

"Huh?"

"You fake-killed me, but the authorities have reopened the case and reclassified me as missing rather than dead." Peyton slumped down in his chair. "No wonder my brother's so obsessed with finding me. All this stuff is tying up a portion of the estate. As long as there's even a chance I'm alive, it screws up his inheritance."

Shay narrowed her eyes at the screen. "I've let this shit go on far too long. Don't worry, Peyton. I'll take care of this. I've got you."

FINIS

My brain is on reserve powers... There's only a week and a half till the first move – yeah, first move. Lots of packing to do while working a day job and writing and (my fave part) chatting with you guys online. I'll be putting everything into storage and moving into extended stay for a month while the new house is finished. (Yes, there's a cancer operation mixed in there somewhere. I'll think about that later) Good news is I'll have a lot less to do while I'm there. We're just gonna stick with the good news.

I don't know that I've felt this tired since the Offspring, who's 30, was a baby. Moving is as hard as it looks but after a year long journey of figuring out where I really wanted to be – I'm almost there!

That's the cool part. No matter where you are, or what your circumstances might be – if it's not quite right (or it's really flaming not right), you can take steps to get to somewhere else. Talk to trusted advisors who will talk to you about solutions and not about what might go wrong. That's not helpful.

I used to think that looking for problems ahead of time was not only helpful, it was necessary. What I wasn't getting was that kind of futurizing was stealing my present-day joy and helping me to overlook what was getting right. My head was turned in the wrong direction.

It also makes it harder to stick with a good idea that's having some hiccups, which means I missed out on good ideas in the past just because I didn't stick around long enough.

New strategy. Why plan for problems that aren't even happening? How about if I wait till they show up, *if* they show up and do something then? Very new thinking for me. Goes against all those business, rah rah, let's win against everyone else books, I know. I'm okay with that. I'm adopting the Anderle method in its entirety. What if everyone wins?

Frankly, if I stick to my journey that's what will happen. Sure, there will be rough patches and outright failures but when they show up, I'll ask for help, take in the data, make course corrections and go on. Like now – all is well, sure I'm a little tired but that'll pass. Just going to keep doing the next right thing in front of me and before you know it, I'll be past the surgery, in the new house.

Just to give some perspective to those who may be looking at where I am now thinking, sure, sure – how hard could it be to go from one house to the next... during the Great Recession there was a time when I was down to a bed, a dresser and two and a half chairs in a small apartment, no car and was diagnosed with *terminal* cancer that time. Things evolve even when it seems like it's happening at a snail's pace. It's still happening, and it adds up. Keep going.

Thanks for taking the ride with me. More adventures to follow.

THANK YOU for not only reading Shay No. 4 (sounds like a perfume to me) but also reading through to these author notes in the back.

I'm writing these notes while waiting for a flight back to Vegas (I'm at DFW Airport). I'm starting them in the Centurion Lounge (American Express) in the D terminal. Apparently, a storm came through and shut down the C Terminal for about forty-five minutes, knocking our flight over to the D (International) terminal.

This week, LMBPN has only two (2) books being published, and they are both "Shay" books. Book 04 comes out in just four days. Unless you are one of the first to read this book, it's probably out already (July 13th this week. No comments about Friday the 13th folks!)

After this week, we have six weeks where we publish a book (planned) all but three weekdays. Something like twenty-seven books in six weeks if everything goes right. I hope we pull this off, as we are setting ourselves up to change how we publish moving forward, and we are going to implement changes this year, in anticipation of next.

The first change we are looking (I am looking) to change is when the $0.99 day(s) are held. Right now, we started doing emails for all books when they publish and *then* sending an email.

We can't possibly do so many emails next year, for both your sake and ours.

So, I'm looking to change our $0.99 days for EVERY new book released that week to Saturday. So, if it comes out on Monday or Thursday, or Friday, it won't matter. It will be on sale on Saturday. I'm looking to do three emails each week. One will announce what is coming out, and give you a chance to set a reminder (I REALLY hope we figure this out) on your calendar when it comes out for Kindle Unlimited (or purchase) during the week, OR to a button to put it on your calendar to remind you to grab the book on Saturday.

If this works as planned, you won't have to worry that you missed a $0.99 sale during the week. You will know that it hits on Saturday.

I have to admit; I'm hoping like hell that this works for you as readers. With such a BHAG (Big Hairy Audacious Goal) as four hundred books in one year, we have to streamline like crazy sonsabitches to not crater our Indie Infrastructure.

We aren't Hachette or one of the big five publishers.... We are LMBPN (the tiny little feisty publisher that can.)

So, changes are coming—ones that I hope get you

MORE excited about our stories and continue to engage you as fans of what we do.

I have more to tell you, but that will probably happen in another book ;-) Until NEXT time…

Ad Aeternitatem,

Michael

- Rule of Magic (4) - Dealing in Magic (5) - Theft of Magic (6) - Enemies of Magic (7) - Guardians of Magic (8)

The Soul Stone Mage Series

* Sarah Noffke and Martha Carr *

House of Enchanted (1) - The Dark Forest (2) - Mountain of Truth (3) - Land of Terran (4) - New Egypt (5) - Lancothy (6) - Virgo (7)

The Kacy Chronicles

* A.L. Knorr and Martha Carr *

Descendant (1) - Ascendant (2) - Combatant (3) - Transcendent (4)

The Midwest Magic Chronicles

* Flint Maxwell and Martha Carr*

The Midwest Witch (1) - The Midwest Wanderer (2) - The Midwest Whisperer (3) - The Midwest War (4)

The Fairhaven Chronicles

* with S.M. Boyce *

Glow (1) - Shimmer (2) - Ember (3) - Nightfall (4)

CONNECT WITH THE AUTHORS

Martha Carr Social

Website: http://www.marthacarr.com

Facebook:
https://www.facebook.com/groups/MarthaCarrFans/

Michael Anderle Social

Website: http://kurtherianbooks.com/

Email List: http://kurtherianbooks.com/email-list/

Facebook Here:
https://www.facebook.com/TheKurtherianGambitBooks/